Adam Andrews Johnson

This book is a work of fiction. The characters, incidents, and dialogue are drawn from the author's imagination and are not to be construed as real.

For information, connect with the author on social media.
Instagram @AdamAndrewsJohnson
Twitter @AuthorQueerotic
Facebook.com/AdamAndrewsJohnson

Acknowledgment

Massive thanks to Claire Rosalind, fellow author of books featuring queer characters, I am so grateful for her encouragement and support while I was writing this book. After she beta-read "The Mantis Variant" for me (another THANK YOU!), I bounced a bunch of my ideas for this sequel off her, and she helped me plot out my story in a huge way!

Jason "Fozzie" Nelson, I love you, boo, and I can't wait until your books come out!

Adam Andrews Johnson

This book is dedicated to Christa and her dreams of destruction.

Chapter 1 – Ninyani

In the northern village of Frostflower, the winter solstice celebration was just coming to an end, but the chill of the season was already smothering the town in its frozen embrace. Snowdrifts were piled up against the sides of houses and icicles hung from every overhang. The evergreen forest that stretched across the surrounding region was also covered in a blanket of sparkling white.

Ninyani always liked the cold. He was born in the village, and the high mountains that surrounded it were his playground. As a boy, Ninyani spent much of his time outdoors, bundled against winter's snap, and he frolicked to his heart's content. He was small, and puberty arrived later for him than some of the other youths. Ninyani's 14th birthday came and went earlier that autumn, yet as the weeks slipped by, he remained childish.

His life in Frostflower was simple. Ninyani was permitted to play after his duties, which most frequently included collecting firewood. During the springtime, he was occasionally sent out on foraging or fishing missions, and those were tasks he enjoyed. Whenever the hunters felled a beast of the forest, Ninyani would be required to assist with the rest of the community in its preparation. The youngest villagers were often tasked with scrubbing the skinned hide of the animal, a job Ninyani did not care for, but he knew what was expected of him. His primary responsibility, however, was to gather wood.

He and his mother lived together in a small cottage. Their home was on a path with several other similar dwellings. She and Ninyani were friendly with their neighbors, and they were close with the members of their community. The older youths often watched over and cared for those who were younger, and Ninyani grew up with many mentors and role models.

Ninyani's mother was a bright woman, with a clever tongue and keen eyes, and she raised her son with love. The two of them spent much of their time talking by the fire at their hearth, which was the focal point of the home. She told him tales and whispered secrets to her son, and the flickering light of the flames made her stories all the more mysterious to his young mind.

Above their home's entrance was a small loft, and up in it, Ninyani made a private space. He slept there and collected little treasures that he found in the surrounding forest. His mother's chamber was below and off to one side from his loft, and Ninyani could see into her room from above. Together, they cooked and tidied their home; they kept a root cellar stocked with foods that they fermented and preserved.

Ninyani and his mother were happy.

Everything that happened in Frostflower revolved around the worship of their living god, Bulog, and the deity walked amongst his subjects. He was an old and decrepit man.

New gods emerged very rarely in the village, and it was sheer luck that Ninyani was alone when his startling god-powers first activated.

On that morning, he ventured far into the frozen woods that surrounded Frostflower. Ninyani was still skinny and childish, but his endurance was impressive. He was a long way from home when he eventually stopped and found a good spot to eat the lunch his mother had packed for him earlier that day.

Ninyani sat down on a stone that the wind blew clear of snow during the previous night, and he unwrapped the food. The root vegetable and sausage cake his mother prepared for him that morning was no longer warm, but he enjoyed a large bite of it. His thermos of tea, however, was still piping hot. He took a sip.

Ninyani was able to enjoy only a small amount of his lunch, before the thermodynamics of the cosmos moved through his fingertips! Every trace of the heat from his tea vanished, and it froze to a solid block in an instant. The expansion of the liquid caused a large crack to split the thermos from its mouth down to its base. At the same moment, as if a raging supernova suddenly blazed to life in Ninyani's other little palm, with a flash, his lunch cake was transformed into a cinder.

He did not comprehend what was happening, and he jumped up and fled through the woods back toward Frostflower. Nothing distracted him, and he raced straight to his home. Ninyani slammed the door, wrapped his tiny arms around his mother's waist, and he burst into tears. He did not know why he was crying; the broken thermos, his burned-up lunch, maybe the confusion he felt, or possibly just his fear of the unknown.

His mother was very worried. "What is it, my snowdrop?" she asked. "What happened?" but he could only sob into her apron. "Are you hurt? What's wrong?" She squatted down with her child, examined him, and she wrapped Ninyani in her arms. She soothed him until he was calm.

Ninyani eventually managed to say between his shuddering breaths, "I did something bad."

"What did you do, my baby?" His mother looked concerned and added, "Whatever it is, we can fix it."

Fresh tears started to leak from Ninyani's eyes, because there would be no fixing it.

"*I broke the thermos!*" Ninyani wailed.

"Oh, no," his mother replied with a relieved smile. "Let me see it."

She rubbed her son's back, as he held up the cracked drink container with the cylindrical brick of tea inside.

"Wow," she exclaimed and asked rhetorically, "how did it freeze like that?" Ninyani's mother was not expecting an answer, but he gave her one.

"I made it cold," he said, "and I burned up my lunch." The boy's face broke into a pitiful grimace, as he tried to choke down a sob.

"What do you mean, my little snowdrop?"

Ninyani rubbed his eyes hard and looked up into his mother's face. "I don't know," he whined.

She pulled him close. "Tell me what happened. Did you leave the top of the thermos open and the cold air got inside? When water freezes," his mother explained, "it expands and gets as hard as stone. Is that what broke the thermos?"

"No, mama," Ninyani replied. "*I* did it. I froze it, and I burned up my lunch," and the boy added, "with my hands."

"Oh, no," she repeated with a chuckle, feeling content that nothing was *actually* wrong, "did something happen to your food? Did you not eat your lunch? Are you hungry?"

Ninyani pouted at her and nodded that he was.

"Okay, snowdrop, let me make you something warm." She set a kettle to boil and started frying up a few fritters for him. A moment later, she set a mug of tea on the table and kissed him on the forehead.

The boy reached out for the steaming beverage with a relieved expression, but then he and his mother were both startled, as the teacup ruptured at his touch.

Ninyani's mother immediately grabbed a towel to catch the scalding liquid and prevent it from pouring onto her son, but there was none. No tea spilled from the broken mug.

At the center of the jagged shards of ceramic was a steaming semicircle, but the tiny trails of vapor that rose from it were not the warmth that rises from a hot beverage. Instead, coiling up from the frozen liquid was the steam of something so cold that it was affecting the very atmosphere around it. The tea was a block of ice.

His mother touched it, but she cried out in pain, and Ninyani jumped with surprise. The woman recoiled and clutched her hand. A wicked burn of frostbite bit into her fingertip and greyed her flesh. Her eyes bulged at not only the pain, but also at the unnatural physical reaction she witnessed. As she wrapped her hand in a warming cloth to treat her frozen fingertip, her eyes widened, and her mind grasped at the truth.

Ninyani was distraught at his mother's pain. He did not understand what was happening to him, and in his nervousness, he picked up his fork to fidget with it. Again, he and his mother were shocked, as the metal utensil liquified. Molten steel dripped onto the tabletop and sent little bursts of flame up from the wooden surface. They licked at the boy's fingers, but he was unburned.

His mother grabbed a pitcher of water. "Step back," she warned, and she doused the superheated metal.

It sizzled and slowly began to cool.

Ninyani's mother took his little hand and they sat together on the floor by the hearth. Long moments passed, and neither spoke. He worried that he was in trouble for breaking the teacup and burning the table. His mother did not clean up the water on the floor, and Ninyani kept looking over at the puddle. Everything felt like it was going wrong for him that day, and he tried to hold back his tears.

However, when his mother spoke again, she did not speak in anger. She whispered words to him with a voice he never heard her use before. She sounded amazed, and her eyes were full of wonder.

"You are our next god."

Bulog, the god of Frostflower, was old. He was blind in one eye and deaf in the same side's ear. When he hobbled around the village, he did so with a pair of canes that helped keep him upright. He gripped them in his feeble, boney hands. Bulog's white beard was long.

The people were obedient in their exaltation and fear of him. With the old god's centennial birthday approaching, more than a decade passed since the most recent deity was revealed and subsequently slaughtered. Ninyani was only a toddler at the time and too young to remember when the old god realized a new goddess was rising. Bulog was made aware of the 13 year old girl, and he demanded that she be brought before him.

Ninyani often heard the villagers tell the story, and they took great pleasure in describing the goddess. With the awakening of her inner deity, the girl's physical appearance began to change. The young teenager developed strange patterned markings across her skin, and her skull started to change shape. Her eyes grew out of proportion with the rest of her face, and her nose developed an aquiline point. They called her the twisted goddess.

Bulog did not possess any physiological abnormalities, and he declared the young girl to be an abomination. Without the opportunity for contest between them, Bulog immediately and totally destroyed the new and potential goddess, and the people praised their lord.

Bulog remained ever-vigilant in his search for the future deity who might replace him.

Many times during Ninyani's childhood, his mother sat him by their fire, and in secret, she told him another side to the story of the goddess. Whenever the soothsayers, or even Bulog himself told the tale of the child's slaughter without a battle, Ninyani's mother would later whisper different truths to her son.

She told him often, "Our god is a wicked man." His mother refused to call the murdered child *twisted*. "That poor goddess, that poor little girl was killed by an old, jealous, petty god. And he is weak! The goddess, she was not a mistake of nature, like others claim. None of the gods are mistakes, you hear me, Ninyani?" his mother would implore. "Not even our living god." She explained the way of deities to her son.

"Bulog is a god of the mind, a god of dreams, and he is not to be trusted," Ninyani's mother informed him. "Bulog does not have his people's best interests at heart. I don't know if he even has a heart. He is cruel and wrathful, but he is a god, and he is not a mistake." She whispered, "He is weak; someday he will be gone, but none of the gods are mistakes."

Ninyani's mother harbored a healthy aversion to Bulog in her son. She also taught Ninyani to keep his feelings hidden. People in Frostflower did not resist their god.

Bulog was intimidating. He insisted that all the children and youths of the village come to him first thing every morning for guidance, and it was little Ninyani's least favorite part of each day. The god of Frostflower would drone on, mumbling about how great he was and how it was right for the people to worship him.

The mandatory time with the 99 year old living god came with very little creativity from the elderly man, and Ninyani often dozed or daydreamed his way through those unpleasant early-morning sessions. The god of his people held no interest for the boy, and Ninyani always sat to Bulog's deaf and blind side. When the children were released, Ninyani would scamper away to do his chores. He found collecting firewood to be far preferable to the daily rants.

On the morning that Ninyani's powers came to life, Bulog's arrogant banality lasted shorter than it sometimes did, and the boy was deep in the forest when the energies of the cosmos exploded from within his body.

Seated beside his mother in their home that evening, she repeated her words in a whisper.

"You are our next god."

She picked up a fresh log and placed it onto the embers of their fire.

"My little snowdrop, can you make that wood burn?" she asked, as if it was the most normal thing for him to do, and he did.

Ninyani reached forward, touched the log, and a raging fire burst from it.

The flames encircled his hand, and his mother instinctively snatched his arm and pulled it from the fire, but Ninyani was again unharmed by the heat.

For the next several hours, his mother tested her son's abilities. He seemed able to access heat and cold on command. He melted more metal for her, froze more liquids, even put his little hand back into the fireplace flames and caused them to die. All through the evening, she experimented with what her son, the god, could do.

As night darkened, Ninyani's mother told him something that he was not expecting.

She inhaled slowly to prepare herself and said, "Our living god, Bulog, is a wicked man."

"I know, mama," Ninyani replied.

"He murdered that little girl, the goddess who came before you."

"I know, mama," he repeated.

"But I've never told you *who* that little girl was." His mother took another breath. "She was the daughter of your mama's best friend. I've never told you about her, because after Bulog killed the goddess…" and Ninyani's mother paused, "her mother threw herself into the gorge. My friend's name was Liahou; her daughter was Poilu, Poilu the goddess." She said their names with sorrow, but also with reverence in her voice. "Poilu would have been one of your caregivers, but Bulog killed her outright for being a threat to him."

"I know, mama."

"He is weak," she continued, "and he killed her without a battle, because he knew that she would have defeated him in combat. That's the way it's always been; battle is the means by which a new god replaces the old, but Bulog denied Poilu the chance. He was not ready to give up control, not ready to lose his throne or his realm."

Ninyani's mother thought to herself that if the goddess replaced Bulog a decade prior, Poilu would have ended up being the one who Ninyani would have been obliged to challenge. She pushed the thought of what might have been from her mind. As fate would have it, Bulog was the only thing standing in Ninyani's way to the throne of Frostflower.

His mother looked at her deity-son with amazement, but there was also fear in her expression. She could hardly believe what she was about to tell her son to do. The boy was still such a child, but the dormant god within the 14 year old was awakening, and Ninyani was leaving boyhood behind. His mother looked into her son's eyes, and tears now began to pool in her own. Throughout the evening, she was too full of wonder to understand what everything truly meant, but it was slowly coming to her.

"Are you okay, mama?"

She reached out and cupped his cheeks. "Ninyani, my little snowdrop," she said in a gentle voice as her tears began to trickle, "you need to *kill* Bulog."

The boy did not comprehend and stared at her with a blank expression.

"You know he is our god, but you also know that he is wicked. I've told you."

"Yes, mama," Ninyani confirmed.

"You've heard the stories from long, long ago," she continued, "about when Bulog was a boy, how he killed the old god who came before him, and how he's killed many of the rising gods since."

"Yes, mama." Ninyani wiped away one of her tears and asked, "What is it, mama?"

The woman said to her child, "He is going to kill you. You must kill him, or he will kill you. You, Ninyani, are our next god. *You* are the new god of Frostflower, but there is only one way to ascend the throne, and that is to take it from Bulog."

Ninyani's mother continued. "The gods are not mistakes," she said to him, repeating words she said many times before. "You are not a mistake, just like Bulog is not a mistake, but it is now your time, and god must replace god. Do you understand me, Ninyani?" She did not wait for his reply. "The new god *needs* to replace the old god. Bulog is the old god. Do you see? It is your duty to remove him. There is no mistake. This is who you are, and the time is right for the old god to be replaced by the new, but he is a fearful and weak old man. You cannot trust him to allow you to challenge him."

She took her son's hands. "Please, my little snowdrop, you must do this," she pleaded. "This is who you are. Now is the time." Then she told him what to do.

For generations, the people of Frostflower only ever worshiped a single living god, and their histories did not tell of a time that came before. The gods of their past had been praised until each was replaced, when a new god possessed powers that were strong enough to end the previous god's reign. Few of the infrequently-born gods were ever given the opportunity to reach their full potential.

New gods were a mystery, and there was no way for the villagers to know who among their youths might have a dormant deity living within them. Even Bulog could not determine from which child the next god would emerge.

There was nothing special about the people of Frostflower. They were mere humans, one and all, except for their god. The people did not know the reason why gods were born from time to time, and none of the fairytales they made up could explain the phenomenon.

Traditionally in Frostflower, when any new god was revealed during the onset of puberty, the rising child would be presented before the reigning god. Then the two would do battle.

However, that was not what Bulog did with the most recent child-goddess, and Ninyani's mother was determined to protect her son.

Frostflower was covered in the night's darkness, as the boy stepped outside.

Unlike the mere mortals who were Bulog's subjects, the old god did not believe he could die, not until another god rose and he was slain. His people, on the other hand, lived with human fear of their own death, but their god was certain it did not apply to him. Despite the ravages of time and old age, Bulog *knew* that he would live forever, and no guards were ever required to protect the sleeping deity.

Ninyani was terrified, but under the direction of his mother, he crept unseen into the building adjacent to the village meetinghouse. It was his least favorite place in Frostflower, and now he entered of his own free will and approached the reclining form of the people's living god.

Bulog slept on a large bed in the middle of the room. Candles and incense gave the space an ethereal feel, and Ninyani always disliked the aromas that Bulog burned. The boy crept around, stood behind Bulog, and leaned forward over him.

The old man was snoring quietly. He looked skeletal in the gloom.

Bulog was born in the year 151 AE, and he was on the verge of his 100th birthday. The villagers spent several days preparing for the festivities, but their god's centennial celebration would not come to pass.

The story of Bulog's rise was often recounted when the people of Frostflower gathered in the meetinghouse for meals or communal time. At the age of 12, it was revealed that Bulog was the next possible replacement for the god who reigned before him. Other potential gods had risen through the decades, but none was ever mighty enough to usurp the old god.

Young Bulog was brought before the people's living deity and told of the battle that was to commence the following day. However, that night, Bulog assassinated the old god while the village slept, and his name was forever lost to history.

The next morning, there was only Bulog, and the people worshiped him for over 80 years. Like each god before him, during Bulog's reign, several youths rose up as new deities, but all challengers were defeated.

In the silence of Bulog's bedchamber, Ninyani stood over the sleeping god. The old man's wheezing snores were the only other sound in the quiet room, except for the pounding of Ninyani's heart in his ears. The 14 year old boy was afraid, but he could feel *it* within him, the godhood. Ninyani did not comprehend the nature of his abilities, but they were as natural to him as breathing.

After his mother experimented with her child's powers, she told him how to use them on Bulog.

Ninyani brought his palms to either side of the sleeping god's head.

His mother had comforted her son, informing him that it would be peaceful for the old man to die in his sleep, and Ninyani tried to convince himself that he believed her. She told him that he would be releasing and setting free the deity who dwelt within Bulog's failing body.

Ninyani stood quietly and felt the powers within him. Then the new young god did as he had been instructed. Ninyani unleashed his manipulation of temperature into Bulog, and the old god neither moved nor flinched as his life disappeared. He did not awake, and he did not open his eyes. His limbs remained still, as his energy slipped away.

The young god simultaneously subjected Bulog's head to the physics of temperature transference, both as an object of extreme heat, and one of deep freeze. He poured the energies of a star from one hand, and with the other, Ninyani controlled naught-temperatures that were like a black hole of cold. He consumed any trace of heat from Bulog's head, while also subjecting it to a blaze stronger than fusion.

The old god died.

Between Ninyani's open palms, Bulog's shoulders, neck, and head turned to ash. They crumbled. The bed was unburned and the rest of Bulog's body remained intact. The horrible remaining flesh of the god's corpse did not bleed. It was cauterized, and smoke and steam rose from the hideous gory mass.

Ninyani looked at it. He jolted to the side, and the boy vomited hard. His guts poured onto the floor of the dead god's bedroom. Ninyani coughed and clutched at his stomach. A moment later, he caught his breath and rose. He tried not to look at Bulog's remains, but something sparkled in the dust that a moment ago was the old god's head, and Ninyani found a small gem.

Whatever fear the boy felt was temporarily overshadowed by wonder, and he gently pinched the glittering stone between his thumb and first finger. It was uncut, an irregular crystal, and no bigger than the tiny iceberries that the people of Frostflower cultivated during the brief summer months. Ninyani sealed the gemstone inside his coin pouch and slipped it into his pocket.

Then his anxiety returned, and he fled from the dead god's house. He raced straight back to his home and his mother, but on his way, he was surprised to encounter a person lying in the street who seemed to be asleep. Then he passed a second in the same state, but Ninyani could think of nothing except returning to safety.

He wanted to forget what he just did, wanted to go back to being a little boy, back before the god within him awoke. Ninyani reached the front door to his home, threw it open, and rushed inside. He was panting and tears were again leaking from the corners of his eyes, but his mother was not in the main room of the house or in her bedroom. Ninyani called out but received no answer.

It did not take him long to find her, and the boy was very startled by her state. His mother was contorted in a strange position at the bottom of their cellar stairs. It appeared that she fell, and she was not moving.

Ninyani crept down to her. "Mama, are you okay?" he whispered into the shadows.

His mother did not reply.

Ninyani raised his voice and cried out to her, but she was dead. He wailed in sorrow, as he touched her cold skin. The blood in her veins held no warmth, and her face was grey in the dark basement.

Sobs wracked little Ninyani's body, and he sat long minutes beside the corpse of his mother, before rising and again climbing the stairs. He stood at the top and listened. The house was too quiet. Ninyani knew that he could not stay there a moment longer, and he rushed to the door and ran outside again. He crossed the path to the neighbor's house, but it was also silent. He knocked and called out but no one responded. Ninyani opened the front door, and he screamed.

Right inside the doorframe, three bodies were lying together. It looked like they had just poured themselves each a glass of wine, and suddenly dropped dead. Candles burned, but everything else was still. The bottle and glasses were strewn around the corpses.

Ninyani sobbed as he trekked from one house to the next, to the next. It took him all night and into the early morning, but he eventually found each villager, including quite a few who were sprawled on the cold streets. Every single person was dead. As the sun began to slide up the sky, Ninyani was the only living soul in Frostflower.

This was not what he expected. This was not what his mother told him would happen.

Ninyani did not know how to be a god. He did not know if he could even be one with no subjects. The boy always believed his mother's words, but now, he was not even certain that he really was a god.

In sorrow, the boy returned to his home and his dead mother. Ninyani had no idea what would become of him★

Chapter 2 – Vion, Part One

Sunrise stretched over Teshon City, but within one of the Messiah residences, there was no movement. No one stirred. None of the five people who fell asleep in that dormitory the night before, now awoke with the morning.

Behind a thin veil of grey clouds, the sun crept up the winter sky. The city below began to stir, and the people started their daily activities.

However, inside the Messiah residence, the five bodies remained unmoved. The hours slid by, and it was not until sunset that another of their fellow Messiahs visited the house.

He stepped up to the front door, knocked, and called out, "Hello?! It's me, Vion! Is anyone in there?!" but he received no reply, and he headed around to the back. There was still no sign of his companions, so the Messiah looked at the top of the two-story building. He squatted down, then leapt with ease up onto the slanted rooftop.

Vion peered through a window, but the sight that befell his eyes shocked him. He slipped and almost plummeted from the roof. The fall would not have injured him, but he caught himself and again approached the glass. He could not believe what he saw.

Vion slid open the window and the vile stench of rotting flesh and scorched hair hit him in the nostrils. He staggered back, retching and covering his face. There were two other windows that he could access, and he opened them both to air out the communal bedroom.

Vion could not tell which body belonged to each of his now-dead friends. They were all horribly destroyed. Two of the bodies were little more than skeletons, each a sickening shade of green, and much of their flesh was melted. One of the bodies sizzled with tiny sparks of purple electricity that crawled across its epidermis, which was now charred and blistered. The final two were like crystalline shells of themselves. Their appearance was similar to a cicada's husk, shed in summer. They were almost transparent and just as delicate.

Vion wrapped a scarf around his mouth and nose, and he forced himself to enter the repulsive room. He reached out and touched one of the clear shells that was still in the shape of a person, but it began to crumble. Vion could not cry; he could barely react at all, and he stood staring from one ruined body to the next. When the stink made his head start to spin, he climbed back out onto the rooftop. His nose and mouth felt polluted from the repulsive air, and he spat and snorted. Then he balled his fists and wailed his despair at the darkening sky.

His sorrow-filled brain barely comprehended the information his senses gave him. Vion fell to his knees on the roof and sobbed into his hands. His best friends were dead. Those people who were closest to him, his brother and sister Messiahs, they were gone.

Less than an hour later, Vion was back at the front of the residence. He was standing behind the Principal Messiah.

She unlocked the door and entered.

Vion and four of the woman's officers entered behind her, and they all headed upstairs toward the large shared bedroom. The horrid stench was overpowering and two of the Principal Messiah's crew with weaker intestinal fortitude ran back down and outside to be sick in the street.

Vion coughed through the scarf that covered his mouth and nose, but he managed to say to the Principal Messiah, "Let me be the one to find out who did this, and I will bring the killers before you for your justice." Tears welled in his eyes, and he added, "They were my friends." His gaze moved over the bodies.

The Principal Messiah dry-heaved and waved for them all to return downstairs. They joined the two already out in the street, pulled down their face coverings, and tried to catch their breath in the clear air.

Vion and the Principal Messiah's eyes met. She said to him, "Do it. Find out who killed them. I bestow upon you the title of High Truth Seeker. Chenchi and Proge," she said to her two officers who stayed with them in the room, "you will be my inquisitor lieutenants. Aid Vion in discovering who is behind this massacre of our people."

"It shall be done," replied Proge. He was not a large man, but he was a Messiah, and size mattered little to the empowered. Proge was also a stern individual, who smiled rarely and exuded a seriousness that was so infectious it was almost viral. His dour expression possessed the power to ruin moods.

Chenchi also responded to the Principal Messiah. "Yes, milady." Chenchi was a burly woman with thick thighs and muscular arms. Her hair was long and straight, and she wore it twisted back in a severe bun. She turned to Vion. "What are your first orders, High Truth Seeker?"

Vion looked at his two lieutenants. "As much as I hate to say it, I think we need to examine the room and the bodies. Maybe we can dab some scented oil onto our face coverings before going back in," he suggested.

With several drops of neroli on their scarves, the three reentered the house and climbed the stairs back up to the gruesome bedroom. Proge rushed over to another window that was still sealed, and he slammed it open.

"Let's each…" Vion started, but he coughed in the foul air. "Don't talk. Go out when you need to," he finished. He pointed at the beds, then for long minutes, the three did not speak.

Vion knelt between the two transparent husks of his friends. Much of one was already crumbled to dust from when he touched it before, and he leaned close to the second body to examine it. He did his best not to bump the bed or disturb the fragile remains. He could not tell who it was. There was no hair on the pillow, and the victim's skin tone was now nonexistent. Vion realized that he could even see translucent organs and bones inside the shell. He turned to the other body. Its chest and part of its head were now dust, and only the arms and legs were still intact.

His two inquisitors examined the other remains. Chenchi was leaning over one of the green-boned and melted bodies, while Proge knelt beside the one that still crackled with electricity. He reached out to touch it, but before his fingertip even came into contact with the scorched flesh, the purple sparks rushed to his hand and blasted him away. Proge slammed into the wall and fell to the floor.

Neither of his companions bothered to look over at the electrocuted Messiah.

Chenchi brought her hand to the scarf over her mouth, holding it tight to her face as she spoke. "The bodies are booby-trapped," she declared.

"I don't think so," replied Vion. "I touched this one earlier and it started to disintegrate." He coughed at the putrid air.

Chenchi pulled a large knife from its sheath at her hip and gave one of the melted bodies a tentative poke. Nothing happened. She tapped the flat of the blade against the green skull's forehead, and it rang out in the quiet room. The bones were solid.

Proge pushed himself up. "Fucker shocked me," he said.

There were no longer tiny volts of electricity crawling across the charred body.

"What could've done this?" he asked, looking at the other corpses.

"Only one thing," Chenchi replied.

Vion stated what she was thinking. "Shifts."✪

Chapter 3 – Memories

After the vast devastation of the underground one year prior, very few Biological Shifts were willing to remain beneath. Most moved to the Gate Town district, and in particular Shifton, which was safest for Shifts. A neighborhood watch was formed to help keep the new inhabitants of Gate Town safe from those who would hunt them.

Gate Town was always the most welcoming part of Teshon City, but the inhabitants of Shifton were now wary of outsiders. There used to be an unsaid understanding that if Shifts stayed among their own kind and kept their powers secret, they would be safe.

Everything was now different.

Biological Shifts were out; they were out of the underground and living in the tight-knit community of Shifton. There was no denying that Shifts were part of society.

When the Biological Shifts first arrived in Gate Town, they did not expect to be welcomed. However, their Shift cousins and many allies who already dwelt in Shifton were accepting, and they embraced their new unusual neighbors.

It was not uncommon to see Biological Shifts with animal-like qualities or characteristics. Many grew thick coats of fur or hair all over their bodies. Some were scaly like reptiles, and still others possessed appearances that were unique unto themselves.

Along with the Biological Shifts becoming part of society, there was a new boldness in a majority of the Shifts who had been living in secret. Seeing their physiologically different kin living out and proud in Teshon City, with the sun shining down on them, Shifts all over Gate Town began to use their incredible abilities out in the open.

Everything was different.

*

Dozi awoke in the darkness. She yawned, stretched, and rolled over to try and steal a little more sleep. Rustling noises indicated that she was not the only one beginning to rise, and she begrudgingly opened her eyes.

First, she saw the familiar pair of shadows sit up together in the dark, then she heard their voices. The two whispered to each other, and their words were no more than quiet hissing syllables when they reached Dozi's ears.

Dozi liked sleeping in, and she was not ready to face the day, especially not this particular day. She was very fond of the little group that she had cultivated over her first year and a half in Teshon City. The strays she gathered were a family.

"Good morning," Dozi mumbled to the other two. She pushed herself up and lit a few candles.

Ilya gave her a bleary smile.

Tchama blew her a kiss.

"Are you two ready for breakfast?" Dozi asked them. "We are supposed to head to the mystic's this morning." She looked at Tchama. "I know you didn't know her, but you are still welcome to come with us, and Lahari just adores you, so that's enough of an excuse."

"Thanks," Tchama mumbled with a toothy grin.

She and Ilya rose and made their way into the kitchen. They whispered in sleepy tones to one another, as they began to poke around in the cupboards.

Dozi turned her back to them and began to dress in her layered and bulky clothes. Most mornings, she woke up in a positive mood. She loved her life in the city, and she had grown quite close to those whom she now considered family.

On *this* day, however, her upbeat feelings were overshadowed by the date.

It was already a cold winter, and Dozi dressed in several layers, taking her time. She allowed herself to experience the feelings that were washing over her, but she did not expect her emotions to be as strong as they were. When she was dressed, Dozi stood alone in the main part of her basement home for a moment, replaying those few memories; there were not many, but they were strong.

She listened to the other two young women clanging around with a few pots and pans, then the smell of bacon snapped Dozi's attention away from her thoughts, and she joined the other two in the kitchen.

They enjoyed several strips of bacon and one hard-boiled egg each. Dozi sprinkled hers with salt. Ilya dipped her egg in hot sauce, and Tchama wrapped hers in one of the rashers. When they finished eating, the three crept out through the hidden entrance behind the old industrial fan cage.

The late dawn of early winter was slowly breaking over the sleepy city, and a brisk wind blew in off the waters of Teshon Harbor. The three women headed inland, away from the tip of the peninsula where the mystic's shop used to be. He now lived in a small house with his daughter and his husband in Shifton.

Dozi, Ilya, and Tchama walked beneath the Messiah temple on their way across town. After the rescue battle one year ago, the uppermost roof of the pavilion ended up collapsing. There was also a cave-in below the Tower that caused its massive doors to sink partway below the street level, and the structure now seemed much less impressive.

The three young women continued along, and soon they entered Gate Town. They stopped at a bakery and a bell rang as they opened the door.

A man called out, "G'morning!" He gave them a little wave with a floury hand and continued kneading the dough on the counter in front of him.

"Prinkleberry or plain?" Tchama asked Ilya and Dozi.

"Well, Theolan does prefer the prinkleberry," Ilya commented.

"But the plain one looks particularly good today," Dozi added.

The baker chimed in, "Them prinkleberries are at the absolute peak of ripeness! If'n you all like'm, now's the time to be enjoyin'm."

The three looked at each other and Tchama nodded. "Done!" she declared to the man with a bright smile. "We'll take the cake with prinkleberries, please."

He wiped his hands on his apron, carefully removed the dessert from the display case, and placed it into a box.

Dozi gave the man more than the amount listed, and he smiled wide at her as they left.

"Have a nice morning!" he called after them.

The three turned down a street and Tchama shifted her gaze back out toward Teshon Harbor.

"Dark clouds are gathering," she commented.

The two others looked at the sky.

"Looks like rain," Ilya replied.

"It's about time," Dozi added.

The winter rains were still yet to fall on the city.

As they passed an alleyway, a door swung open and four drunken men came shambling out. Their eyes landed on the young women and they stumbled over to them.

One put his arm around Ilya's shoulders and looked up at the tall woman. He mumbled, "Never had me a girl azzz big azzz you before. How big are ya, girl?" He turned to his companions. "Hey, fellas, how big izzz she?"

Ilya was taller than all of them.

Two of the belligerent men trapped Dozi between them. She was mortified, and the stink of their breath made her recoil, but she was firmly stuck.

The final man tried to lean in and kiss Tchama's cheek, but she pushed herself away from him.

"Watch it!" she snapped. "Why don't you just leave us alone?!"

"We don' t'ink we will," he slurred at her. "We t'ink you's t'ree should come with us. We's been partying all night long, ain't we boys? And we's ain't finished yet, is we?"

The inebriated quartet laughed lecherously at the three young women, and Dozi tried again to shake the two men from her.

She urged the group towards the mystic's home. Their destination was at the far end of the street and still many blocks away.

"Where d'ya think yer goin' off to?" said one of the men at her side, and he grabbed her arm.

The other one asked, "What's yer name, girlie, huh? You can call me *uncle*." He stuck out his tongue and waggled it very close to Dozi's face.

The man who tried to kiss Tchama snatched her wrist, and the cake wobbled in her grip.

"Stop!" she cried. "You're gonna make me drop it!"

He guffawed at her and slapped the box from her hands, sending it flying across the street.

"No!" Tchama yelled, and she wrenched her forearm out of his fingers. She ran to the fallen box and knelt beside it.

The men cackled like hyenas. They pulled Dozi and Ilya over so they could leer down at Tchama, and Ilya suddenly found herself in the same situation that Dozi was trying to escape. There was still a drunk man firmly stuck to one of Ilya's sides, but then the man who knocked the cake to the ground wrapped his arm around her waist. She and Dozi were each sandwiched between two men.

Tchama lifted the cake box's lid.

The decadent treat inside was smashed.

Then, right behind all of them, a voice yelled very loudly, "*Good morning!*"

The inebriated men jumped with a start, and Dozi and Ilya managed to slip from their grips. Everyone spun around as the voice spoke again.

"Oh, dear, did that lovely cake fall to the ground?"

It was the mystic and his husband. They wedged themselves between the men and women, and both of them took their time giving Dozi, Ilya, and Tchama long hugs. The mystic then turned to look at the men. He was shorter than all four of them, but he stared up with a defiant smile.

"Isn't that just a shame," the mystic said in a voice that was thick with sarcasm. "Looks like there was a terrible accident. I wonder if it's salvageable. Come along, girls!" he called out. "Thank you, gentlemen," he added in a droll monotone, "for all your help. We can take it from here," and the four befuddled drunkards were left standing in the street.

A moment later, Dozi, Ilya, and Tchama entered the mystic's and Theolan's home.

"Lock the door," he said in a serious tone, and his husband secured the house. "We are done dealing with those fools."

However, the handle rattled and fists pounded against the outside of the door.

"*Hey, girls!*" hollered one of the men. "We weren't done with you yet! Let us in!"

From upstairs, a familiar voice called out, "I've got this!" and Lahari descended. She unlocked the door, opened it to the men, and the very unique woman stepped into their midst.

The four staggered back in shock, but she grabbed one of them by his face.

Lahari's yellow eyes were glowing in the early morning sunlight, and the black spines that grew out all over her body were raised like a wicked halo.

The man squeaked a small noise that may not have been loud, but there was no mistaking its meaning. Fear, anguish, isolation, torment, woe, suffering, misery, terror, and the crushing empty void, all were in his pathetic whimper.

Lahari pushed him and he crashed into his drinking companions. She did not say a word, as the men stumbled over each other and could not get themselves away from the scaly blue-skinned woman fast enough. They lumbered down the street, unharmed, and disappeared into an alley.

Lahari closed the door and turned to face everyone with a satisfied grin. Many of her expressions were indistinguishable behind her unique visage, but her smile was bright.

"I guess I'm glad you didn't do what I was expecting," Ilya commented to her.

"What do you mean?" Lahari asked.

"Well, as you opened the door, I thought, *she's going to kill them.*"

Lahari smiled again. "Threatening seemed like enough." She stepped up to Tchama and wrapped an arm around her in a side-hug.

Once they were calm, Theolan asked the others, "Can you believe it's already the anniversary? It's been an entire year."

"This morning," the mystic added, "I told Lahari that when you three arrived, I just knew I was going to burst into tears, but that chaos out front distracted me. Let's start over," he suggested. "It's so wonderful to see you all! Let's have some *proper* hugs," and each of them embraced the others.

He turned to Tchama. "Now, why don't we take a look at the damage? What do you say, my dear?"

"It's ruined!" she whined, as they all gathered around the kitchen table, and Tchama opened the box.

Juices from the red berries were streaked and speckled all over the pristine white frosting and spongy vanilla cake, both of which were mangled. The prinkleberries that had decorated the top and were hidden as layers within, now made the cake look like the bloody scene of a murder.

"I think this looks absolutely delicious!" the mystic said with a beaming smile.

Tchama pouted. "It was so pretty."

"Not to worry, my dear," he replied, tapping her on the nose, "we will still enjoy it! Of that, you can be sure!"

Tchama then asked him and Theolan, "You don't mind that I came along for the party, too, right, even though I didn't know her?"

Theolan replied, "Tchama, we love that you are here! You've become a very special member of this family, and it feels like you've been with us for a lot longer than just since this past summer. You're one of us."

Lahari then stated quietly, "I try not to think about her too much," and everyone else fell silent. She continued. "Remembering Agrell makes my heart hurt. I miss her," and that was all it took.

Tears began to flow. The five shared memories, and even though Tchama never met Agrell, her eyes also welled up at the outpouring of emotion from the others. They laughed and cried, and when they were ready for it, each of them enjoyed a chunk of the mangled prinkleberry cake. It was most delicious.

Dozi, Ilya, and Tchama stayed with the mystic, his husband, and Lahari for that entire day. They celebrated the one-year anniversary of the death of their friend, each sharing their impressions of the special person they knew for mere days. Agrell had impacted them profoundly.

Theolan and the mystic prepared a home-cooked supper, during which plans were made as a group. With the winter sun beginning to set, the three women headed home again.

The following morning, after a good night's sleep, everyone was back at the mystic's house.

"I cannot *believe* you all convinced me to do this," Dozi declared to the others. "I have not once wanted to go back since arriving in Teshon."

"But don't you miss your old friends and family?" Tchama asked her.

Dozi rolled her eyes. "Of course I do, but I expected my life to be so full that I never needed to return home. And it is," she added. She looked around at each of them and mumbled, "Can't believe you're making me do this."

"We aren't *making* you do anything," Theolan replied. "We really don't have to do it if you are seriously opposed to the idea."

"No, it's not that," Dozi replied in a dejected tone. "I just don't have any desire to go back to that tired old village. I spent my entire childhood looking forward to leaving it."

"But this is going to be fun!" Tchama declared with enthusiasm.

"Yeah," Theolan concurred, "I'm also looking forward to this. I think it'll be good for all of us to get away from the city for a while."

With packs on their backs, and bundled against the elements, the six of them left through the Oselian gates and made their way beyond the Teshon City outskirts to Bloodwater Crossing. The bridge over the Lonely River was old but sturdy, and it spanned the short distance across with the raging torrent below.

"Have any of you ever been to Ilin?" the mystic asked as they approached a sign for the ruins.

"I did once," Dozi replied, "when a group from our village came down to the city for supplies. The old fort is kind of pretty."

"It's weird that none of us have ever visited it," Theolan commented, "even though it's so close to town."

"There's not much to it," Dozi added.

The mystic replied, "Why don't we go see them? The ruins can be the first sightseeing stop of our trip."

"Well, there's not much to sightsee for the rest of the journey to Bluewood," Dozi informed them, "so enjoy this."

They came to the minor trail that branched off the Pinewood Path, and the group followed it. After a very short walk, they approached the old castle, but then they were stopped.

"That'll be one copper coin each to visit the ruins."

Several people stepped out onto the path in front, but also behind the travelers.

"Highway robbery, is it?" the mystic asked in a chipper tone of voice. His response took everyone by surprise. "I have exactly what you're looking for here in my bag," he added, and he flipped it open. "Look, let me show you," and he tilted his satchel, as he stepped toward the people in front of him.

A jingling sound made them lean forward.

Out of the mystic's bag launched a small purple orb of thin glass. It shattered against one of the robber's jaws and sent a shimmering cloud around the others' faces. They coughed and clutched their throats before falling to the path unconscious.

The mystic turned on the people behind, and he removed two more glass spheres. He smiled. "Take your friends and go," he said in a jolly voice. "Take them, or else things are going to get worse."

The remaining thieves hesitated, looked at their unconscious companions, and they decided to let their would-be targets go on their way.

With the ruins of Ilin in view, the travelers turned their backs on it and returned the way they came.

When they were again on the Pinewood Path, Dozi said, "Maybe this is a bad idea and we should just turn back. I wish Agrell were still around for moments like that."

"Not to worry, we're not helpless," the mystic informed her.

"Yeah," Lahari added, "if it came to it, I could have disintegrated all of them." Her voice was slightly muffled by the thick scarf that kept her face hidden.

"Yikes," her father replied, still grinning, and he continued. "That was exciting for a moment, but I suspect we won't be seeing many people, if any, until we reach Bluewood."

"You're probably right about that," Dozi agreed. "I didn't see anyone on the entire journey when I moved away."

Tchama pulled her jacket tight against the cold and asked, "Remind me again why we decided to do this now; why didn't we wait till summer?"

Lahari pulled the scarf away from her face and answered. "I wouldn't have been able to make the journey with you." Every inch of her unique skin and each of her unusual spines was hidden under the layers of winter clothes. Dark snow goggles concealed her yellow eyes and helped to keep her secrets secret.

For a while, the group walked along the Pinewood path in silence.

"Some of this is going to be a little bit of a hike," Dozi warned the others, as they approached the first rise of the foothills that led to the mountains.

For a few hours, they climbed, until the sun began to slide down toward the horizon. The group found a spot off the path to make their camp, and as Ilya assembled two thick tents that would protect them against the elements through the night, the others collected firewood.

Ilya liked living with Dozi and Tchama in the hidden basement home, but venturing into the wilderness to enjoy some solitude had become an important part of Ilya's life. Even though she did not need any protection against the elements because of the powers of her photonova gland, she took to using a tent for the comfort it provided while she was in nature.

By the time the others returned from the nearby forest with the firewood, their sleeping arrangements for the night were already assembled. The group lit a fire and cooked stuffed sweet potatoes that the mystic had prepared for each of them before they left the city. They were all exhausted from their long day of hiking, and they ate in silence.

Darkness covered the land, and even with the fire burning, it was a cold night. One by one they made their way into the tents, and soon they were all asleep.

The journey took a further two days of hiking, and their travels brought them high into the forested mountains. On that third evening, with the sun setting behind them, they reached Bluewood Village.

Torches were burning at the entrance to the town, and as the group approached, they were greeted by a watchman.

"The night's getting dark," he called out, "and you lot have traveled a long way. Welcome to Bluewood. Can I point you toward the tavern?"

Dozi stepped up to him and pulled her scarf down. "It's me," she said, as if that clarified everything, and it actually seemed to do just that.

"*Dozi!*" the man cried, and he wrapped his arms around her. "I truly thought you would never come back to visit us! Your mother and father are going to be so excited," he declared, but then his face fell, and he looked worried. "Oh, they're not here," he told her.

Dozi scoffed and repeated his words in an incredulous tone. *"Not here?* Why are they not here? Where are on earth they?"

"There's been three attacks," the watchmen stated. "Three children have been taken."

The mystic spoke up with his voice full of concern. "Taken? Taken by whom?" he asked.

"It's not a *who,*" Dozi answered. "It's a what," and she turned back to the man. "Was my brother taken?"

He shook his head. "No, but a boy was snatched this evening, and your parents are out helping to find him."

"Let's get settled at the pub," Dozi recommended to the others, "then I can tell you all about it."

They left the watchman at his post and Dozi led the group to the inn. Several enthusiastic individuals in the tavern were surprised to see Dozi, and they greeted her as the group entered. All of them insisted on also welcoming each of her fellow travelers to Bluewood Village. Lahari stayed bundled for the salutations, but it was not long before the group from Teshon City was in a private suite.

Once they were behind a closed door and Lahari was free to disrobe, the unique Biological Shift woman stripped off everything. The rest of the group could not help but watch her. She flexed and stretched, and her quills moved in mesmerizing patterns across her scaly blue skin. She was quite a sight to behold, and her father beamed at her.

Theolan wrapped his arms around the mystic and said to his husband, "Your daughter is quite beautiful."

Lahari glanced over at the pair with a spiny-faced smile. "Thanks, dads," she replied.

"Now, listen," Ilya interjected, and all eyes turned to her. "I think I should fly up before it's too dark, and see if I can spot the missing kids."

"It's already too dark," Dozi replied.

"No," Ilya retorted, "I'm going to fly up and see what I can see."

Dozi rolled her eyes. "Fine! Do what you want. You're almost as noble as Agrell."

"Aww," Theolan said in a soft voice, and he repeated, "Agrell."

"I'm going," Ilya declared.

"We'll head down to the tavern and bring food back to the room," the mystic told her. "We will be here."

Everyone but Lahari left and returned to the first floor. Ilya went outside, as the others entered the pub.

A few minutes later, they were back in the room with Lahari, but before the food arrived there was a knock on the door.

Ilya called out, "It's me!"

They let her in, and she looked frightened.

"Something's on fire!" she declared.

"What do you mean?" the mystic asked.

"In the opposite direction of Teshon City, there is a huge column of smoke stretching up toward the sky."

"Opposite of Teshon City is north," Dozi replied in a dismissive tone. "That's the highlands. There isn't anything up there. There's nothing to the north."

"Well, something's on fire!" Ilya implored. "It's too dark to tell what it is, but I want to fly to it and see what's happening."

"No!" Dozi replied. "Please, don't do this."

"You know she's going to," Lahari responded.

Theolan then recommended to Ilya, "Have a little food with us before you go. It should be here any minute."

"No, I'm going now. Just give me another one of those dried fruit and nut bars that you made for us to snack on during the journey, and I'll be fine."

The rest of them realized that there was no changing her mind, and Theolan handed her the bar.

When the door closed behind Ilya again, the mystic asked, "Now, Dozi, what happened to the children from your village?"

"Yes, please, tell us," Theolan implored. "What took the children?"

Dozi turned to the others with a serious expression. "The last time one came down from the shadow peaks, I was just a child. It ended up taking seven children back then. I was one of the lucky ones."

"But what is this monster?" Tchama asked. "What is it, Dozi?"

Dozi took a breath. "It's an icewyrm."★

Chapter 4 – Gawa, Eroli, & S'Kay

A trio of unusual individuals sat huddled around a small table. Each of them was unique. They spent several moments in silent awe, only occasionally breaking the quiet to express their feelings.

Three mugs of dark beer sat on the tabletop.

A woman with skin like mineral-rippled marble said, "It worked. It actually worked." She looked like she was made of movable stone, and the strange patterns on her skin moved in continuous and fluid swirls. There were no visible pupils or irises in her colorless eyes, and her scalp was smooth.

"It was incredible," agreed a man with thick hair the color of wheat, which covered every inch of his body. Long claws extended from his fingertips, but he retracted them to lift up his glass for a sip.

The third individual remained quiet for the longest. She was bird-like in her appearance. Tiny protrusions curled up from the backs of her arms, over her shoulders, and across the sides of her face. Like the other woman, she did not have hair, but there were larger extensions on the top of her head that looked like feathers.

"This is only the beginning," she finally said to the other two. She turned her eyes to one of them and then the other. "I fucking love you both," she declared. She stared into the eyes of the woman made of marble and said her name. "Gawa." Then the bird woman turned and gazed into the eyes of the hairy man. "Eroli," she said.

Eroli said back to her, "I love you." He stroked the thick fur that covered his collarbones and chest.

"I love each of you," Gawa added.

The bird-woman smiled. "I already can't wait to do it again," she said.

Gawa whispered to her, "I love you, S'Kay," and Eroli repeated her.

"I love you, S'Kay," and S'Kay smiled at them both.

Gawa said, "I can't believe our first time went so well," but she paused. "Wait a second. No, I take that back. I actually *did* believe we would be that good. I know we said we should wait in between times," she added, "but I don't want to wait. I want to do it again, and I want to do it soon. I don't know that I've ever felt more alive than when we were done."

Gawa sighed and continued. "The three of us, just standing there together in the dark, being quiet and reveling in the moment," she said wistfully, "I feel like that's what my life is meant for; that's my purpose."

The bird-woman and beast-man were smiling, and S'Kay added, "I could not imagine my first time without you both."

"I've never felt more alive," Gawa repeated. The rippling pattern on her skin shifted in its ever-moving flow.

"And you were beautiful," S'Kay added.

"I actually think that it's a good idea for us to wait just a little while in between," Eroli started to say, but S'Kay interrupted him.

"I don't want to wait," she said in a demanding tone. "I think we should do it again tomorrow!" She spoke over whatever protests he attempted to make. "And we can do it without you next time, if it comes to that. We're going to do it again, with or without you, Eroli."

"Yeah," Gawa agreed, "I don't want to wait either. I want to feel that alive again."

Eroli looked at the two women with uncertainty. "I guess if you want to," he ventured, "I guess we don't have to wait. I already know the perfect second place." He paused and asked, "Do you both really want to do it again tomorrow?"

S'Kay and Gawa smiled.

Each of them took a sip of ale.

S'Kay caressed the feathery wisps that grew from the back of her arms, and she said to the woman with skin that looked like stone, "Gawa, tell Tualu that we need him again tomorrow night."

"It'll be my pleasure," Gawa replied. "We make a good team, the three of us and him. I suspect our little group will grow over time, but I don't want to risk compromising what we have by inviting anyone else to join us yet."

"I agree," S'Kay concurred. "Maybe after we do this a few times together, we'll decide to invite someone new to join in, but I don't see that happening for a while. Did you have someone in mind?"

"No, not necessarily," Gawa responded. "I guess a few folks pop up, but I'm not in a rush to add anyone else. There will be a better chance of getting caught if there are more of us. Our first time was so impressive, and I wouldn't mind a few repeat occurrences before we bring in new people."

"*People?*" S'Kay repeated with a smirk. "As in, the plural of *person*? It seems that you have a few people in mind indeed," and she finished with a laugh.

Gawa smiled and simply said, "I'm excited for our next time." She held up her hand and examined her palm. It glowed purple as the patterns shifted across her skin.

S'Kay shook her feathers, licked her smiling lips, and said, "We are going to accomplish such amazing and terrible things."✪

Chapter 5 – Ninyani & Ilya

Ninyani stayed at his home in Frostflower, even as the body of his mother putrefied at the bottom of the basement stairs. The 14 year old boy did not know what he could possibly do. He was small, and there was nowhere else he could go.

During his days alone, he scoured every building in the village for any signs of life. He found none. Ninyani did see several of the forest's wild crystal dragons, but only on the first two days. With no people left to keep the traps armed, there was nothing to stop the beasts from slinking through the town in search of prey.

Each year, a few children were taken by the dragons, but it always happened out in the surrounding woods. The guards of Frostflower prevented the monsters from ever entering the village itself. However, the beasts now crept down the narrow lanes and sniffed at each house; they did not find what they sought. Despite Ninyani's confidence that he was a god, he stayed hidden from the crystal dragons while they were there. They did not stay long, and once they were gone, they did not return.

Ninyani spent his waking moments searching the village and eating whatever food he could scrounge or throw together. He was already a skinny boy, and the limited amount of prepared food meant there was little for him to eat. He cried often, and would fall asleep in different places, waking in terror and confusion as the reality of his predicament came crashing back to him.

On his 11th morning in the dead village, the horrors finally pushed the young boy over the edge of his misery, and Ninyani inadvertently set his village on fire. He did not mean to cause the inferno, but his sorrow was like an avalanche, and it covered all other thoughts and feelings. He did not realize that the god-powers of thermodynamics within him had ignited the pile of logs beside his home's hearth, and in an instant, the room was ablaze.

The tests that his mother worked through with him when they experimented with his powers were far from Ninyani's mind, and instead of stealing the heat from the flames before they could spread, the boy fled. He reached the edge of his village and watched the fire leap from one home to the next, until all of Frostflower was in flames.

The buildings burned as the winter sun slid across the sky. It slowly began to set, threatening the land with oncoming darkness, but the raging flames of Frostflower illuminated the forest with an eerie light.

Everything that Ninyani knew in the entire world was swiftly being turned to ashes before his eyes. He could not think. He could not cry. He could only watch the devastation. Smoke billowed toward the winter sky, and it looked like streaked charcoal that an artist smudged across a painting of dark clouds.

Night fell, and still, the village burned.

From the darkness above his head, Ninyani heard a voice speak. For a moment, he thought that he must have died in the fire, and Death was there to claim his soul. However, the words spoken were not how Ninyani expected Death to sound.

The voice called out, "Hey, are you okay down there?!"

Ninyani scanned the smoky skies, but he could not see who was speaking.

He was not dead, and he wondered if the voice came from inside his own head. *Am I hearing things?* he thought.

"*Boy!*" the voice called, clearly coming from outside of his head, and Ninyani looked up again.

A woman was hovering in the air near the tops of the trees, and she was looking down at him.

"What happened?" she asked above the roar of the flames. "Where is everyone else? Why are you alone?"

Ninyani started to cry and fell to his knees. He looked up through his tears, but the woman was gone. Maybe she was just a figment of his imagination. He dropped his face to his palms and sobbed.

Then a hand touched his back and the same voice spoke right beside him.

"It's going to be all right," she said in a gentle tone.

He looked up and asked between shuddering breaths, "Who are you?"

"My name is Ilya," she replied. "I saw the smoke. There are some missing children from Bluewood Village, and I thought they might be near the fire, but this place is much farther north than I realized. I don't think the children could've gotten all the way up here. What is this place and what happened? Where is everyone?"

"*They're all dead!*" Ninyani wailed.

Ilya was not expecting that. "Who's dead?" she retorted. She took Ninyani's hand. "Come away from the fire," she urged, and they moved a little farther into the trees. "How can everyone else be dead? Did they die in that fire?"

"No," Ninyani replied pitifully, "they've been dead."

Ilya furrowed her brow. "What do you mean, for how long? How did they die? Are you sure there's no one else?"

Ninyani took a ragged breath. "They died when I became the new god."

Ilya did not know what that meant. "Erm... What's your name?" she asked.

Ninyani opened his mouth to speak, but he hesitated and took a breath. Then he replied to her.

"I am Ninyani, living god of Frostflower. The old god before me is dead, and I am the new god."

Ilya was more confused. "You think you're a god?" she asked him.

Ninyani looked uncertain, but he said, "I am."

"What do you mean? Why do you think you're a god?"

"Because I can do this."

He reached down, picked up a twig, and it turned to ash in his fingers.

"Oh!" Ilya responded in surprise. "You're a Shift?"

The boy gave her a blank expression.

"I'm a Shift, too," Ilya informed him. "I can fly! You're not a god," she said with a smile, "you're a Shift."

Whether out of sorrow, or fear, or exhaustion, or hunger, or despair, or offense at words that would have been described as *blasphemy* by the villagers of Frostflower, the boy attacked her. Ninyani grabbed Ilya's forearm with both hands, and he poured his heat and heat-absorption into her flesh.

"*Hey!*" she snapped. "What are you doing?"

Rage was scrawled across the boy's face, or maybe it was terror, or woe, and he lashed out at the only living person in the vicinity of his burning village. However, instead of ruining Ilya's flesh and turning her arm into a cinder, like his powers did to the old god's head, Ilya wrenched her forearm out of Ninyani's little hands; she was unharmed.

She put her palms up, facing him in a gesture of surrender, and said, "I'm not going to hurt you. You don't need to be afraid of me. In fact, I think you should come with me." She waved toward the flames. "You can't stay here, and now that I know the lost children from Bluewood aren't here, I think we should head back. Come with me," she urged.

The boy looked at his burning village and fresh tears sprang to his eyes. "I'm sorry!" he wailed, and Ninyani wrapped his arms around her.

"It's okay, it's okay," Ilya comforted. She spoke in a kind voice. "I don't know how you were raised here, but you shouldn't use your powers to attack people. You're a Shift. Don't use your powers against others."

Ninyani wiped his eyes with his sleeves and repeated himself. "I'm sorry." He blinked hard. Then he looked up at Ilya with an expression of wonder and asked her, "You... you can really fly?"

"You just saw me flying," she reminded him with a smile. "Here, wrap yourself in my jacket." She removed her outer garment, and the boy stuck his skinny arms into sleeves that were much too big for him. Ilya buttoned the coat and pulled up its hood. "It gets cold," she warned.

"But won't you be cold?" Ninyani asked.

"Temperatures don't affect me," Ilya informed him. She squatted down. "Now, wrap your arms around my neck and hold on tight."

Ilya stood, and the two of them lifted off the ground. She needed to soar high into the sky above the forested mountains in order to see the lights of Teshon City in the distance. As she approached it, she knew that she would eventually be able to see Bluewood Village, but the city was her target.

She flew through the dark winter sky with the boy in her arms. The wind whipped around them and the leagues passed below, and as Teshon City approached, the flickering of lights in the forest alerted Ilya to the location of Bluewood Village. She circled it once and opted to land on the Pinewood Path just outside of town. Ilya and Ninyani's feet touched down, and they approached.

When the watchmen saw them round the bend in the trail, he waved and called out his greeting.

"I'm Dozi's friend," Ilya informed him. "I was out trying to help find the lost children, and I found this boy who is *not* from Bluewood, but he was alone.

"Oh no, did you get lost," the man asked Ninyani. "Are you hungry?" and the boy nodded to him.

"I'm going to bring him to the tavern for food," Ilya said to the guard. "One of our group is a healer. I want him to look the boy over."

"That's a good plan. Do you need me to guide you to the inn?"

"Thank you," Ilya replied, "that would be very kind of you."

They followed the watchman and arrived a few minutes later. He left them at the front door to the pub and resumed his duties.

"Come on," Ilya said, "let's take you to the room so you can meet everyone, and we can get you some food."

She climbed the stairs with Ninyani and knocked on the door to the private suite.

"It's me," Ilya called.

Tchama opened the door.

"Hey, everyone," Ilya said, as she and the boy entered. They closed the door behind them. "I didn't find any of the lost children from Bluewood, but the smoke that I saw was coming from a separate village very far to the north." She looked at Dozi. "It was *way* up north over an enormous mountain range, much farther away than I first thought. I can sort of understand why your people don't know about it." Ilya turned back to the others. "The entire village was on fire. Every building was burning, and this boy was the only person there. I'm sorry," Ilya added, turning to him, "please, remind me of your name again."

"Ninyani," he said in a quiet voice.

Ilya turned to the mystic's husband. "Theolan, can you please run down and order Ninyani some food?" she asked.

"Absolutely," he replied with a smile.

Lahari's voice called out from the second room, "Ilya, I can't hear you! Sorry, do you mind saying it all again? What happened with the smoke?" and she stepped into view.

"*Monster!*" Ninyani shrieked, and he pointed at her with his eyes bulging and a look of sheer horror on his face.

"Whoa, whoa!" Ilya responded, stepping between Ninyani and Lahari. "I'm so sorry," she said over her shoulder to the unique Biological Shift woman. "Do you mind waiting in the other room for a few minutes while I explain things?"

Lahari bristled and gritted her teeth, but Tchama took her by the hand.

"Please," Ilya begged, "I'm so sorry, Lahari. I don't think he's familiar with Bio-Shifts."

The spines all over Lahari's body flexed a little, as she allowed Tchama and Dozi to lead her into the other room.

"Ninyani," Ilya said gently to the boy, "that's Lahari. She is a Shift, like you and me, but unlike us, her body changed. She's not a monster. She's our friend."

Ilya turned to the mystic. "Will you look over Ninyani?" she asked. "I want to make sure he's not hurt." Then she said to the boy, "Let him check you out. He's a healer and will know if anything is wrong."

She entered the second room and closed the adjoining door. Tchama and Dozi were flanking Lahari.

"I think he's kind of like Agrell," Ilya stated, hoping the memory of their lost friend would help soften Dozi and Lahari to the plight of the boy. "From the tiny amount I've gathered, it seems like the people of that village actually thought Shifts were some sort of gods. He told me he was made to kill the previous god, who I think was just some poor old Shift man. Ninyani said because of going through that, he was the new god." Ilya paused before continuing. "But the entire village was on fire. There were no people anywhere. I don't know what happened, but he was not interested in staying."

"I don't fucking trust him," Dozi replied, and she crossed her arms over her chest. "Maybe *he* burned the village to the ground. If he's a Shift, maybe he killed everyone and started the fire."

Ilya shrugged. "He did attack me when I first landed, but I think he was just scared. He didn't seem to actually want to hurt me. Whatever he's been through must've been terrible."

Dozi frowned at Ilya, but then Tchama commented to her, "We're a pack of strays."

Dozi turned and snarled at hearing words that she spoke often, now being repeated and used against her.

Tchama added, "He should be one of us, and besides, you took *me* in." She smiled sheepishly at Dozi and Ilya.

"Ugh!" Dozi grunted, rolling her eyes at the three of them. "Fine!" She threw her hands up. "We'll give him a test run," she conceded. Dozi sounded annoyed. "You both really bring out the best in me," she said in a voice dripping with sarcasm.

Dozi turned to Lahari. "I suspect the boy will alter the plans for our vacation, and this little old rural village is not as accepting as the city, but at least we are aware of the existence of Shifts." Dozi looked toward the door that led to the other room and the boy who fancied himself a young god. She continued to Lahari, "During the height of the day, the rest of us should still do our sightseeing outside of town, even if your father opts to stay here with the boy." Dozi turned back to Ilya. "I suspect you're right. I would not be surprised if there are strong similarities between him and Agrell."

Theolan came through the door and joined his stepdaughter and the three other women in the adjoining room. "Ninyani appears to be uninjured," he informed them. "I ordered food and it's on its way for him, and I think your dad is going to try and see what information he can gather," he added to Lahari.

"We should give them some privacy," Ilya recommended, "and spend our evening in here."

"That's a good idea," Theolan replied.

Lahari stepped up and wrapped her arm around him in a side-hug. "I'm happy just staying in," she said, "but why don't you four go down and see if there's any entertainment in the tavern?"

Dozi looked doubtful.

Lahari leaned her head on her stepfather's shoulder. "Maybe you'd bring me something," she asked in her most cutesy voice. "I'd love an ale!"

He smiled at her. "Of course, I'll bring one up to you," he replied, and he and the others left Lahari alone in the room.

Like she did at the seaside tavern in Brokenpointe one year earlier, Lahari doused the lights and positioned a chair by the window. She looked out at the dark trees and the star-speckled night sky with her bright yellow eyes.

Maybe I am a monster, Lahari thought to herself, and she chuckled.

A moment later, the door creaked open and her stepfather entered. "Here you are, my dear," Theolan said, handing her the beer. It was dark. "The barkeep says this is the town's speciality, and it's only available during the winter. Said it was a lucknut porter. I ordered one for myself, too," he added with a smile. "I hope you enjoy it, and I hope they bring us both luck!"

"Well, you better get back down there, before someone else drinks it," Lahari replied with a grin. She took a sip. "Ooh, it's good!"

Theolan kissed Lahari on her spiny cheek, left her in the dark with her drink, and he returned downstairs.

The mood in the pub was somber. Those villagers who spent the day searching for the snatched children were exhausted and downtrodden. Almost no one spoke, and the clinking of cutlery was the soundtrack in the background.

Ilya was the only one in their group who ordered food, since the others ate upstairs in the room. The four sat quietly, enjoying their beverages and waiting for the meal to arrive. Soon it did, and Ilya tucked in; they ordered another round of drinks.

When the group was almost finished, one of the Bluewood Village watchmen burst into the tavern. Blood was smeared across his jacket.

"What happened?" called the barkeep.

The man's face was ashen, and he said in a frightened voice, "In the woods, I found half..." he paused before continuing, and he swallowed hard, "*half* of one of the children."★

Chapter 6 – Vion, Part Two

Gate Town was the most welcoming region of Teshon City. The neighborhood at the entrance was made vibrant by the diversity of its inhabitants, the colorful murals that were painted on the outsides of many buildings, and the unique shops and taverns that catered to the Shifts who lived there. The cold winter wind that blew in off the harbor did not stop the inhabitants of Gate Town from being out and about under the grey sky.

Near the small region that bordered the industrial district, and above the old Oselian airstrip, Gate Town was hosting its morning market. Farmers from the area surrounding Teshon City gathered together each day to sell their produce to the gathered crowds.

The market was busy as Vion and his inquisitors entered.

He began to shout.

"With the authority bestowed upon me by her lordship, Eccoodia Aruckleon, Principal Messiah of Teshon City, I hereby declare that the investigation to find the Shift murders of five Messiahs is now open.

People started to congregate.

"If anyone has any information regarding the murderous Shifts," Vion continued, "the Principal Messiah would be very grateful of you sharing it. We know that the murderers are Shifts, and we will find them."

Someone in the crowd shouted, *Get the fuck out of Gate Town!*"

"Messiahs are murderers!" yelled another.

"No one here is telling you shit!" cried a woman.

A voice farther back jeered, *Cannibals!*"

Most of those in attendance at the market were angry, and they were surveyed with suspicion by Vion and his two officers.

"I demand that my authority be respected!" he bellowed.

The woman in charge of the market stepped up and said, "Your authority doesn't reach this far, and respect is the doppelganger of honor. No," she continued, "you will be receiving neither respect nor honor here, and I think it's time you leave. You are not welcome."

There was no way for the trio of Messiahs to know who they were up against, especially in a huge crowd of people at the edge of the Shift neighborhood. There was a strong possibility that they were far outmatched. Quite a few of the individuals gathered before them looked ready to kill the three Messiahs and be done with it.

Vion's fury raged below the surface, but he kept it buried. *Who do these people think they are?* he thought to himself. He knew the crowd would be made up of some humans, who he viewed as less than Messiahs. The presence of Shifts was also a certainty here in Gate Town. Vion even told himself that there might be a few ex-Messiah traitors among them. He scowled at the gathered masses, who not only blocked his way farther into the market, but also denied him access to the entrance of Shifton.

"Murderers are living among you," he called out, "and I came here to keep you people safe by finding them!"

"You people?!" someone snapped.

Vion's inquisitor Proge said to him, "Truth Seeker, it does not seem like this tactic is going to work."

Vion growled but conceded, and the trio turned their backs on the angry mob. They walked away in silence. The neighborhood was bustling and they disappeared among the other pedestrians. Once they were away from the market, no one paid them any mind. The three ducked down an alleyway.

"I can't believe that crowd of degenerates treated us that way!" the inquisitor Chenchi fumed.

"I can," replied Vion.

"But the disrespect was shocking!" Proge added.

"It should be expected with filth like Shifts and those who keep acquaintance with them, but no, this did not go according to plan."

The alley in which they found themselves opened onto a main street, but back in its shadows stood several dilapidated shanties. Bottles clanked and went rolling along the pavement, as a man stepped out from one of the huts. He leaned toward the wall of the alley, brought one of his palms to it for support, and he began to relieve himself. One of the bottles bumped his foot, and he flailed at it, kicking it away. It shattered.

As he turned to shamble back into his makeshift dwelling, he saw Vion and the two inquisitors staring at him from the mouth of the alleyway. Then the three of them heard the man's voice inside their heads, and even in their minds, his speech was slurred.

What're you lookin' at?

The man stepped back into his shack.

"That's a fucking Shift," Vion whispered. He walked into the back of the alleyway toward the deeper shadows. His inquisitors followed him, and when they heard their leader draw his dagger, they both pulled theirs from the sheaths at their belts.

Vion approached the hovel, and he could hear that the drunkard was already snoring again. He slipped the door open and looked down at the sleeping man. Without even glancing back to see if the coast was clear, Vion thrust his knife into the man's neck and yanked it out again.

The alleyway, the man, and Vion vanished.

There was only darkness. Then the dark was replaced by a void.

Vion could see, but there was no light. It was as if he was floating beneath the surface in a pool of water. He was surrounded on all sides by nothing. Above him was nothing, and his feet were standing on nothing. He could feel nothing below him, but he also knew that he was not falling. He was simply standing in place surrounded by emptiness.

A violin began to play in one of his ears, and he turned, but the origin of the sound remained a mystery. Then a child giggled in his other ear, and he turned in the opposite direction. Still, he saw nothing in the emptiness. Then the sound of two stringed instruments in harmony filled the space all around him. He looked everywhere but there was nothing. Then the music stopped.

In front of Vion's feet, a flower grew. It was not strange or unique in any way, and he thought it looked as forgettable as the countless others like it that he had seen in his lifetime, except that this one was growing from nothing. It only stretched up until it was above his ankle, and a bud appeared at its terminal limb that opened with a little yellow blossom. When the flower did not do anything else, Vion tried to walk, but even as he did so, the flower remained the same distance from him.

Vion looked around again, but still, there was only nothingness. Either he was not able to walk forward, or the flower was moving with him, and since there was no point of reference at all, he could not be certain that walking transported him anywhere.

For a moment, he considered reaching down to pick the flower, but instead, he called out into the silence, "Hello?"

His voice sounded muffled.

When he looked back down at the flower again, there were four of them. He did not see the others grow. They were similar but not identical; all were the same species and each was yellow.

Then there were more. Again, he did not notice them until they were fully grown, and several were suddenly behind him. A full ring of flowers circled him, countless little yellow blossoms.

Something flashed in Vion's peripheral vision, and he turned, but there was nothing there. He saw it in a different direction, but again he turned to see only the void. All of a sudden, three little sparkling entities like hummingbirds flitted noiselessly in front of him. They shimmered in rainbow colors, dipping and swirling around each other in the emptiness.

Vion heard a thump. It was so low that he felt it more than heard it. A moment later, there was a pair of thumps, one right after the other. Then the double-beat started repeating. The sub-decibel sounds were slow, and the silence between them seemed to linger. As they continued, they started to grow the tiniest bit in volume. It almost felt to Vion that the non-ground he was standing on was thumping. He could feel it in the soles of his feet.

It almost seemed like the void itself was pulsing. He looked around but the little birds of light were nowhere to be seen. The flowers seemed to be unaffected by the quiet thumping. They neither swayed nor quivered with the sound waves. Vion then noticed that one of the flowers to the side of him was lying down. It looked like it fell to the ground, but because there was no ground, it just hovered horizontally in the void of nothingness.

As his eyes moved, he saw that more of the flowers had fallen over. He did not see them fall, yet they were lying beside their neighbors. Vion did not see any movement at all, but before he knew it, every single one of the flowers was lying still in a ring around his feet.

Little by little, the thumping grew louder but also slower, as if the increasing volume required more effort for each thump.

Then the void around Vion crackled, not with electricity, but with flashes of some entirely different reality. The emptiness returned and remained, and again, there was only Vion in the void.

The flowers were gone.

The bird-entities were gone.

The thumping was gone.

Then the emptiness flashed again, and it began to flicker all around Vion. Glimpses of something else teased his vision, and the nothingness did not last.

The void was instantly replaced by that other world.

Vion was damp. He opened his eyes.

He and the two other Messiahs were down. They were sprawled in the alleyway. Chenchi and Proge were not moving.

Vion pushed himself up from the piss-covered concrete. He was soaked in the drunken man's urine, but also his blood. Within the shack, Vion could see that the man was dead. The horrible wound in his neck still seeped a little blood, but the rest of it was all over the ground. His eyes were unfocused and his mouth hung agape. The man's limbs were twisted in strange angles of pain like a dead insect, and he was motionless.

The Shift's wave of psionic energy that created the hallucination in Vion's mind also blasted both of his inquisitors. They were slowly pushing themselves up from the alley floor.

Chenchi groaned. "That Shift fucked us up," she mumbled.

"I want his fucking head," Vion growled, as he picked up his dagger. He stepped into the shack and grabbed the corpse by its hair. The dead man's tongue lolled out, and Vion cut through the meat of his neck until the head was only connected to the body by its spine. One strong pull decapitated the corpse.

Vion stepped back out of the hut, as his inquisitors were helping each other to their unsteady feet.

"We need to come up with a different method to find those Shift murderers," Vion grumbled, and he looked back into Gate Town, "but at least we got a mantis gland out of this debacle of a mission."

He held aloft the dripping head✪

Chapter 7 – Dozi's Family

Sunrise spread over Bluewood Village, and Dozi rose with its glow. Ilya, Tchama, and Lahari were still asleep. The mystic and Theolan spent the night in the adjoining room with Ninyani, and there was no sound coming from the shared wall.

It was not like Dozi to be awake and alert so early, but she thought to herself that she was more excited about seeing her parents and brother than she had expected. She lay in bed, quietly remembering her father's smile, and wondering how much her little brother had grown in the year and a half since she left.

She wondered if during the day, her parents intended to go back out to aid in the search for the missing children again, or if they would be so surprised to see her that they would stay home. Dozi felt guilty that she might be the cause of making the search party smaller.

The village of Bluewood sprawled into the forest that surrounded it, with lanes that led to cozy little dwellings, and Dozi's parents lived among a patch of evergreens. She spent her childhood playing on a soft bed of pine needles that surrounded her family's home, and she was looking forward to feeling them underfoot again. The trees' scent was also something she missed, and she expected their aroma to be mingled with the smells of food being prepared.

Dozi's mother was a good cook and instilled in her daughter quite a lot of her skills. However, Dozi was very much looking forward to a home-cooked meal that she did not make herself.

In her mind, she ran through the plans for the upcoming day and wondered how much they would change now that Ninyani was with them. Dozi knew that visiting with her parents and seeing her little brother was the most important thing on the agenda, so she intended to do that first.

Dozi would direct the rest of the group to visit the community market after eating breakfast. While she was with her family, the others could spend some time perusing the products that were made by local crafters. She suspected that Theolan and the mystic would find some trinkets or small decorations to bring back to the city.

Dozi considered that Ilya and even Tchama might want to join the continued search for the missing children. She could not imagine what it would be like to lose a child.

Then Agrell entered her mind.

Losing her was like losing a sister.

Dozi shook herself and her mind returned to the day's plans. The others could order food to be delivered to the room and have breakfast with Lahari. Dozi would eat with her family instead, and then meet up with the others afterward. While in town, Lahari needed to be completely bundled up, so Dozi thought that during the afternoon, she could take Lahari out of the village to the watering hole where the children of Bluewood Village played in the summers. The pool was certainly frozen at this point in the year, and the waterfall that fed it was always beautiful.

There were other spots that Dozi considered taking them. The cliff that overlooked the village was lovely. There were also ruins nearby; they were less impressive than Ilin, but they would give Lahari some time free of scrutiny.

Dozi looked forward to seeing whomever from her old crew that she could find. The memory of them made her smile.

The room continued to brighten with the slow winter sunrise.

Dozi was used to hearing the whispered voices of Ilya and Tchama first thing in the morning, but Lahari was the next to rise, and she yawned aloud. Dozi sat up, and the very unusual-looking woman gave her a sleepy wave.

"G'morning," Lahari said to Dozi.

Tchama stretched and squeaked a quiet, "Hi." She nudged Ilya, who groaned and pulled the blanket tight.

Before long, everyone was awake, and Dozi and Theolan headed downstairs. She smiled at him, as she stepped out the front of the inn and left him to order the group's breakfast.

The temperature dropped in the night and there was a brisk chill in the air, but there was hardly a breeze. Dozi was warm in her bulky and layered clothing. A thick knit hat was snuggly on her head and her hands were in a pair of fuzzy mittens. She walked under a layer of gray clouds that hung low in the sky.

The town square was quiet and empty, but before long, it would be filled with lively energy. Dozi did not remember it ever being so quiet, but she admitted to herself that she was rarely up that early. The lane leading to her childhood home was not far, and as she reached it, she felt giddier than she expected. There was a skip in her step, as she made her way along.

Then, there it was. The house in which she grew up looked exactly the way she remembered it. Smoke was curling up toward the gray sky from the chimney, overgrown with ivy. Her father was never keen on pruning, and the foliage often grew bushy on that side of the house.

Through one of the frosty windows, Dozi caught a glimpse of her mother. She smiled to herself again and stepped up to the front of her old home.

A wreath of wrapped blinkwood boughs was hanging from the door. Its little glass-clear berries shimmered like they were made of ice. Several pinecones were attached to the wreath and a tartan ribbon that was tied in a bow hung at its center.

Dozi knocked on the door twice and then turned the handle. "It's me!"

"Hello?" came her mother's startled voice. "Who's there?"

"It's me," Dozi repeated. "I'm here for a visit and I brought some friends."

Her mother looked very surprised.

"But don't worry," Dozi added quickly, "they aren't with me right now. Didn't want to bombard you with a group of strangers."

"Well, that, I very much appreciate," her mother responded, trying to gain her composure. "Now, get in here and close the door. Give me a hug," she demanded, and she wrapped her daughter in her arms. The two women embraced, as clomping footsteps came down the stairs.

"It's not possible," Dozi heard her father's voice say. "My daughter has returned?" He sounded delighted.

Dozi pulled away from her mother and squeezed her father in a tight hug.

She then asked loudly, "Where's my little goblin?" She hoped that her brother would come running, but Dozi's mother replied.

"He's still asleep. He's so stubborn about waking up in the mornings."

Dozi's father chuckled. "Just like someone else we know."

"Come, sit, eat!" her mother implored. "I was just preparing breakfast."

"I can't believe you're here," her father added.

Dozi shrugged. "There isn't really an easy way to let you know ahead of time, so when a few friends wanted to make the trip, I decided it seemed like a wonderful idea. We did get rained on for a little bit of the journey, but it wasn't bad. They're all staying at the inn. I've made some amazing friends, and I can't wait for you to meet them!"

"Well, tell us all about them over an egg and sausage pie." Her mother placed the steaming breakfast in front of Dozi, and she plated up two more.

"I've done pretty well with food," Dozi replied, taking a large bite and continuing with her mouth full. "I cook for myself and my roommates in the city, but I was ready for one of your meals."

Dozi's father and mother sat down across from her with their own pies.

"You've got roommates?" her father asked. "Well, you've never struggled making friends. I'm glad you've built a community around yourself."

"It's been wonderful," Dozi said thickly through a mouth full of food. Each bite was perfection. She felt like it was revitalizing her soul to eat her mother's cooking again, and she appreciated having someone else cook for a change. Ilya and Tchama helped Dozi with a lot of the food preparation, but Dozi cooked everything they ate. Her mother's food in that moment was like magic.

"Last year," Dozi went on, "I made friends with a runaway Messiah, who turned out to be a real hero, also a Bio-Shift, if you can believe that, and one of my roommates is actually a Shift herself!"

Dozi regretted her words the moment they left her lips. Not only did she speak secrets that were not hers to share, but her father's reaction took her completely by surprise.

"You what?!" he suddenly yelled, interrupting his daughter's excited speech. "That's disgusting! We raised you better! Don't you know better? No child of mine is going to live with one of those freaks! What is wrong with you, girl?"

Dozi was speechless.

"You are a disgrace! I can't think of a worse betrayal," her father continued. He turned his scowl from Dozi and looked to his wife for support of his reaction.

Dozi's mother looked appalled, but not toward her husband.

"Who do you think you are?" the woman barked at her daughter. "That freak is here with you, isn't she? You brought her to our town!"

Dozi did not know what to say. She regretted the trip, regretted returning to the backwoods village, regretted bringing her friends, and regretted even more that she divulged their secrets.

"But there are Shift people who live here in Bluewood," Dozi murmured in disbelief.

Her parents looked horrified.

"We don't associate with them!" snapped her mother.

"As far as I'm concerned," her father raged on, "those freaks don't belong in Bluewood!"

"I thought you always wanted to be a Demifae," her brother added in a quiet voice. He awoke at the shouting, and the boy was standing at the door to his bedroom.

Dozi felt a wave of guilt wash over her about the dreams of her earlier life. She learned and had grown so much in her short time living in Teshon City.

"You know how it is," the boy continued. "You know how it works." He was speaking in a calming tone of voice, one he learned to use when Dozi argued with her parents. Over the years, Dozi had argued with her parents a lot. "Only a single Shift needs to die," Dozi's brother quietly reminded her, "for you to be just one in a whole group of new Demifae."

"Shifts are people!" Dozi implored.

"*How dare you?!*" her father shrieked. "I won't stand for those kind of lies to be spread in my house! Do you hear me, girl?" He stood and loomed over his daughter. "Shifts are not humans, and I am shocked, *shocked* that you would speak such a terrible lie!"

Things were already bad for Dozi, but they were about to get worse.

"Daddy," she said in a pleading voice, "why are you saying these things? I mean, I know that Bluewood is just a podunk village, but..."

Dozi did not get to finish speaking her thought, because her father's palm suddenly impacted with the side of her face. The crack of the slap rang out in their little home.

"Not another word, girl," he said in a threatening tone.

Dozi's hands slowly moved to her face. Her eyes were wide and her jaw dropped. They always fought verbally; this was the first time he hit her.

"They're people," she whispered.

"Not another word," he repeated through his teeth.

Dozi took a breath and screamed, *"They're people!"*

"That's it!" her father bellowed. "You're not going back to that corrupt city! No child of mine is going to live with freaks! You're staying here, where you belong."

Dozi unleashed what was inside her and roared, "I knew that coming back here was a bad idea! I left this village and you backwoods people's fear of change! You have a lot to learn. Ugh!"

She pushed past her father and he grabbed her arm.

"Oh, no you don't!" he shouted.

"Get the fuck off of me," Dozi growled, and she tried to pull herself free.

"You're not going back to that city!"

"Oh, yeah, and how are you going to stop me?" she snarled.

He reared back to slap her again, and Dozi set her jaw. She glared at him, daring him to show his true colors again.

She then said in a voice of forced calm, "I'm… leaving…"

Dozi could tell her father wanted to say something else, but when he did not speak or hit her again, she ripped her arm from his grip. Her mother and brother looked shocked, but both remained silent. Dozi grabbed her coat, hat, and gloves and left without another word. She exited the house and slammed the door.

"Ugh!" she roared at the sky, and she stomped back down the path into the village.

Dozi saw Theolan, Ilya, Tchama, and bundled-up Lahari walking through the town square toward the community market. The mystic and Ninyani were not with them. Dozi stayed where she was until the group passed, letting them continue to the shops. When they were gone, she stormed up to their rented rooms at the inn.

Tears were beginning to leak at the corners of her eyes when she entered.

"What's wrong?" the mystic asked in surprise.

"Fuck this place. I'm done here," she snapped at him.

"What do you mean?" he asked in a gentle voice.

Dozi sighed and took a deep breath. "I'm sorry," she said. "We need to leave. My parents are livid that I'm living with a Shift, and they can't believe that I brought her here. I know, *I know,*" Dozi said before he could respond. "I'm kicking myself for outing her. I didn't mean to. We were having such a nice conversation, and it just slipped out, but the reaction was much worse than I ever would have imagined. I don't want to stay here a moment longer," she added.

"I'm so sorry, Dozi," the mystic replied. "Do you want to talk about it?"

"No, I just want to leave." She dropped her head.

"The others went to the market. I don't know how long they'll be gone. Do you want to go get them?"

Dozi rolled her eyes at herself. "Now that I've let it slip that there's a Shift in the village, even though I don't think anyone's going to try anything, I don't want to bring attention to Ilya or Lahari. My parents know there's a Shift here with me, so I don't want anyone to see me with any of *our* people. I just want to leave Bluewood as soon as as possible. I'm going to pack."★

Chapter 8 – Intoxication

At the God's Hole Public House and Tavern, the innkeeper who worked behind the bar was addressed by a customer whose voice he did not recognize.

"Do you know anything about that commotion earlier today at the market?"

The barkeep turned to look at the stranger. "What's that now?" he asked.

"There were some officers who showed up. They were talking about murderers in Shifton."

After Vion and his inquisitors were denied access into the neighborhood, they returned to their base of operations in the industrial district, and Vion changed into his most common garb. That night, he made his way alone back to Gate Town and found a street with several pubs. He entered one and casually asked the owner about the events of that day.

"Heard mention of the disturbance," the bartender replied, "but I weren't there and couldn't tell you what it was about. What'll it be?" he asked.

Vion scratched his chin. "Brandy, neat. Have you heard anything about a group of killer Shifts?"

"I hear all sorts of things in here," the man replied. He poured the beverage. "Don't know nothing about no killers, though. The world's a tough place," he added, "but I reckon they's just rumors. How's your drink?"

Vion nodded and raised his glass to the man.

A group of teenagers at a table in the corner giggled together over a pitcher of mead. An old man with a half-drank glass of wine dozed alone in a booth. A couple of women with several empty glasses on their table were kissing passionately in full view of the other patrons, although no one seemed to be paying any attention to them.

The tavern felt like a bust to Vion, and he left his brandy unfinished, as he turned and walked out the door. He entered the next establishment, but there was only a single customer talking to the barmaid. She was serving a man who was already drunk and mumbling in a loud voice about a lost love. He was saying that everything was his fault and she was gone. Vion growled to himself and left the bar without speaking to either person.

The next pub was down the block and he pulled up his hood to obscure his face as he made his way to it. He yanked the door open and was satisfied to see that quite a few people were inside. Customers were seated at the counter and several tables.

Vion entered and joined the patrons at the bar. He sat between a woman with her back to him and a wizened old codger with a bushy white mustache. When the man smiled, Vion noticed that several of his teeth were missing.

"It's a cold one out there tonight," the man commented in a pleasant way.

The barkeep stepped up opposite Vion and asked, "What ye be 'aving?"

Vion looked at the taps. "Lager," he requested.

"Good choice," said the old man seated next to him.

"Yes," agreed Vion in a dismissive way, and he dove right in with his questions. "Any chance you were at the market this morning? Apparently, there was some sort of disturbance. There was talk of Shift murderers."

The mustachioed old man took a sip of ale. "Now, do you mean *Shift murderers* as in, someone who's murdering Shifts?" he asked. "Or does *Shift murderers* mean Shifts who murder?" He chuckled to himself.

The bartender set a mug of pale beer in front of Vion and said, "A few people were in 'ere talking 'bout the market earlier. Don't rightly know what all was involved, but them folks were in a right tizzy." He paused and added, "They said something 'bout some killers or something."

"Yes!" confirmed Vion, more enthusiastically than he intended. He took a swig of beer, then he added in a normal tone, "That's what I heard, but no one who I've asked has known anything more about it."

The bartender replied, "Let me check with some of the other folks," and he headed down the bar.

"It's a tough town," the old man beside Vion said in a conversational manner. "I was born and raised here, meself, but Teshon's always been rough. Stabbed someone once when I was a younger man, can't remember now for the life of me what that was all about. Ain't been in a fight for some years now, but I used to scrap in my younger days." The man's voice held almost a wistful tone.

A moment later the bartender returned and informed Vion, "There's a woman down at the end of the bar who says she was there, but she's already pretty wasted, and you're not likely to get much information out of her."

Vion nodded. He thought to himself that this confirmed it; the people who lived in the neighborhood were indeed talking about his appearance at the market that morning, even though no one he asked seemed to know about the murders.

The barkeep suddenly put a pair of shots on the countertop, one in front of Vion, and the other in front of the fellow beside him.

"Tove, there," he said, "he just ordered you each a mushroom bourbon." He gave Vion an apologetic shrug. "Enjoy," he added in an uncertain tone.

The old man was beaming at Vion with a gap-toothed smile.

"Tove?" Vion asked.

"That's me!"

The two raised the tiny glasses, clinked them together, and knocked back their bitter beverages. Both of them coughed after they swallowed, and the old man laughed aloud and thumped Vion on his shoulder.

"Blah, that stuff is foul," Vion declared.

"But it gets the job done!" Tove hollered.

The drunken woman at the far end of the bar made an enthusiastic whooping noise of agreement in response to Tove's boisterous outburst, and he gave her a thumbs-up.

Vion smacked his lips. "What did he say that stuff was?"

Tove did not answer him. "Next up," he informed Vion, "we're having a spicy infused whistlewhiskey!"

The hours of night slipped away, and Vion was very inebriated when he finally stumbled down the streets that led to his home. The winter sun was already starting to rise, and he shielded his eyes. The front door to the large dormitory-style building was not locked, and he pushed it open. He stumbled toward the couch, collapsed on it, and passed out in a drunken stupor.

Morning crept toward noon, and Vion eventually awoke in a haze. The sun was gently glowing behind a thin layer of gray clouds, but to his hung-over eyes, it was blazing and horrible.

The clock informed him that it was almost midday.

The house was silent.

Vion lived with 18 other Messiahs in the large housing unit located in western Teshon City. The place should have been bustling, but no sounds came from upstairs, and the kitchen appeared to have been left unused that morning. Vion could not come up with an explanation for the calm state of the place, but he was appreciative of it. The alcohol was hammering the inside of his head.

He rose to his unsteady feet, approached the stairs, and pulled himself up to the second floor. His eyes were unfocused and his stomach was churning as he stepped into the hallway.

Two mutilated bodies lay sprawled in front of him✪

Chapter 9 – Gawa, Eroli, S'Kay, & Tualu

"We're going to do it again," said S'Kay, and her feathers fluttered.

"The three of us were magical the first time," Gawa added in a fawning tone. The mineral-rippled patterns flowed across her unique skin.

"I can't wait until Tualu gets here so we can start," Eroli added. Now that the moment was upon them, he was feeling much more enthusiastic.

S'Kay, Gawa, and Eroli were in a section of the underground that was still accessible. Warning signs around the area declared that it was unstable and that people should keep away. Their hidden space did not collapse during the devastation the previous winter, and the three Biological Shifts now sat together, waiting in the darkness. Only a single candle burned, and its pathetic light did almost nothing against the overpowering shadow.

Eroli was the first to see their fourth companion. "Ah-ha, Tualu! There he is!"

"He certainly knows how to make an entrance," S'Kay added.

"I can't see him yet," Gawa stated.

Eroli pointed and said, "There."

In the air behind Gawa, an almost imperceptible glow began to add its illumination to the candle's tiny flame.

"He's so beautiful," Gawa said in a breathy voice.

The glow increased and began to solidify, and it was geometrical. The new light became the form of shapes upon shapes that overlapped and wove together like a tapestry of angular elements. Then, within the brilliance, Tualu materialized and the light vanished.

"Hello, Tualu," Eroli said to him.

S'Kay smiled. "It's time."

"Tualu, you are perfection," Gawa added. She stepped up and placed her palm against him.

Nothing about Tualu's appearance was human-like. S'Kay, Eroli, and Gawa were all humanoid in form with two arms and legs and a head atop their shoulders. However, Tualu's mutation caused a physical development of his body that fused him with metal. Much of what used to be bones and organs and muscles and flesh was replaced by interwoven mechanical pieces all working together in an impossible and intricate dance that equated to his life as a Biological Shift. Tualu did not have limbs or a head. The man was a large and rectangular machine.

"Hey, baby," Gawa said to him. She turned to look at the other two. "Ready?" she asked.

S'Kay and Eroli stepped up to Tualu. They also placed their hands on him, and the four of them vanished.

In the empty darkness of the underground, the flame of the single candle flickered and slowly burned down until all the wax was melted and the wick died.

S'Kay, Gawa, and Eroli reappeared without Tualu. The brilliant flash that accompanied his appearance was also not part of their arrival. The three of them were holding hands, standing together in a dark bedchamber. A lamplight outside shined through a window and cast an eerie glow into the space. They looked around, found everything that they were expecting, and they released their hands.

S'Kay, Gawa, and Eroli turned their backs to each other.

The west Messiah house was a large building in the industrial district, and it was home to 19 Messiahs, including Vion. He was the only one who was not at home when S'Kay, Gawa, and Eroli appeared in the stillness. All but two of the other residents were asleep.

Before the trio, six Messiahs lay in five beds that took up most of the dormitory-style room.

S'Kay approached a bed with two people sleeping side by side in it.

Gawa stepped between two beds and reached out to the individuals asleep in each.

Eroli's vicious claws extended, and he whispered, "Death to cannibals."

The three Biological Shifts unleashed their cosmic energies into the unconscious Messiahs, who awoke in terror but were unable to cry out, as each was slaughtered by powers they could not resist.

The pair in bed together tried to get away, as their flesh began to melt. They pulled from S'Kay, but both collapsed as hideous green skeletons. A thin trail of steam rose from their bodies.

Two of the Messiahs sat up in their beds, but they fell back and went rigid, burned to human-shaped cinders by Gawa's purple lightning. Flashes of her electricity crackled across their scorched frames.

Eroli sank his claws into the other two, and their lives were extinguished. Their bodies were transformed into statues that appeared to be made of crystal shards. The human form of each was still intact, but they were almost completely transparent, and what remained was as delicate as glass.

S'Kay licked her lips.

Gawa's eyes were sparkling.

Eroli smiled.

The trio approached the door and waited, listening, but they heard nothing. They crept out into the hallway and entered the second room. There were again five beds, but three of them were empty.

S'Kay walked in alone and stepped up to the two sleeping Messiahs, as Gawa and Eroli continued down the hall without her. She again activated her incredible abilities and slaughtered the two Messiahs. They awoke in horrible agony, as S'Kay's powers changed the state of the very matter that made up their bodies.

Her victims could not scream, as their lungs melted inside their chests. They could not see because their eyeballs had liquified. They tried to move before their life left them, but the flesh sloughed from their green bones and steamed towards the ceiling.

Every single one of S'Kay's countless feather-like protrusions possessed the capability to release her energies.

A moment later, she withdrew her hands from the ruined bodies.

They were dead.

She entered the third room behind Eroli and Gawa. Each of them was pouring their energies into two Messiahs at the same time, but there was a fifth sleeper in one of the beds. He awoke with a start and fell to the floor with his sheets twisted around him. S'Kay pounced upon the man and he let out a single wail before her brutal energies destroyed his flesh.

The trio of Biological Shifts heard a door open down the hallway and they peeked out at it. A couple, both in a state of undress, came stumbling out of one of the dorm lavatories. They were looking around in concern. The woman was trying to button her blouse, but it was open and one of her breasts was exposed. The man's pants were unfastened and there was a bulge in his undergarments.

"What the..." he began to say, but his words were cut off, as Gawa rushed at the two of them and grabbed both by their faces. They tried to push away from her, but it was too late, and her violet electricity raged into their bodies. The pair of corpses slumped to the floor, and she left them burned down to charred husks. Purple lightning rippled over their scorched frames.

The three Biological Shifts left the bodies in the hallway.

There were two remaining rooms with sleeping Messiahs. Within each, four of the five beds were occupied, and the trio of vigilantes massacred those who slept therein. When every Messiah in the house was slain, the three crept down the stairs and exited through the back of the building.

S'Kay, Eroli, and Gawa escaped into the city streets in the dead of the night★

Chapter 10 – Ninyani & the Mystic

In preparation to leave Bluewood Village, the mystic was packing his and Theolan's possessions into their travel bags. Theolan was still at the market with Lahari, Ilya, and Tchama.

Ninyani spent the morning with the mystic, and he was feeling comfortable with the jolly man. Having a full belly of breakfast sausages and eggs was also helping, and it made him enthusiastic to talk. He was seated on a lounge chair in the corner.

"What's an icewyrm?" he asked the mystic.

"I'm not actually sure," he replied to the boy. "It seems to be some sort of reptile from the mountains that comes down to take children."

"Oh, you mean a crystal dragon!" Ninyani replied with a smile. He was delighted to know something that the man did not.

The night before, the mystic and Theolan did not ask Ninyani many questions. They sat with him while he ate, and the two men told him a little about themselves and the four women in the adjoining room. Not long after finishing his supper, Ninyani had fallen asleep.

"Crystal dragons are a nuisance in Frostflower," he explained to the mystic, as the man folded a few shirts. "We set traps all around the village to protect us from them, but they still eat a couple of kids each year. I can teach people here how to make a trap for them, but someone needs to guard it at all times."

"Wow," the mystic responded, surprised by the boy's knowledge, "how does the trap work?"

"The only thing that can pierce a crystal dragon's skin," Ninyani continued, "are the bones of another crystal dragon. We use the ribs to make a trap that drops onto them from the trees. We use their leg bones in dragon-holes; dragon-holes are pits that we dig in the ground with the sharpened bones sticking up. We cover the pit with branches and snow so the crystal dragon doesn't know it's about to fall into it." Ninyani then looked like he forgot something. "And we even use the teeth as tips for our spears, and their claws for knives.

"Interesting," the mystic replied, "I'm not sure that it would be possible to build those traps around Bluewood, but that is all quite amazing, Ninyani." He sealed one of the travel bags. "Would you like to tell me more about your village?"

Ninyani nodded.

"Frostflower is home to a living god. Bulog came before me, and I was the new god." Ninyani's memory of his dead mother came crashing into his mind, and the boy fell silent. He had shed so many tears for her already that he did not think he possessed any more. "They're all dead," he said in a quiet voice. "Everyone is dead. Even my mama is dead," and the tears did again flow.

Ninyani leaned against the mystic, who hugged the small boy. He comforted him with reassuring words, but they meant nothing to Ninyani in that moment.

The mystic told him everything would be okay, but in light of the boy's losses, the man knew that the phrase was hollow.

Ninyani sobbed for several minutes.

As he calmed down, he apologized. "I'm sorry."

The mystic squeezed him. "Not at all, my young friend. Are you okay? Do you want to talk more?"

Ninyani nodded that he did.

"Okay, why don't you tell me more about..." he paused. "What was it, Ninyani? I'm sorry, I can't remember the name of the old god."

"Bulog."

"*Bulog*," the mystic dutifully repeated. "Can you tell me about him?"

Ninyani nodded again. "Bulog was the god of dreams. He walked among our sleeping minds, visiting us beyond the realm of the waking world. Our god was an old man when I replaced him." The boy fell silent again.

"How did you replace him?"

Ninyani did not respond.

The mystic decided to redirect. "I think we have a place you can stay, down in the city. I'm sure it's going to be much different from your home, but there are good people down there. And yes, there are some bad people," the mystic added, "but the good folks tend to stick together."

"If our old god was a man," Ninyani said, his mind still on the previous topic, "does that mean I'm not really a god? That's what the flying woman said."

The mystic rubbed the boy's back and informed him, "You fell asleep early last night, and Ilya told me about your conversation. Have you ever heard of Shifts before she mentioned them to you?" he asked.

Ninyani shook his head *no*.

"If I'm not mistaken," the mystic continued gently, "that is, in fact, what you are. You're a Shift, just like Ilya. Your village must've been so isolated that your people were not aware of the history of Shifts."

The mystic's voice took on a tone of wonder as he continued. "Shifts are amazing people who are born with incredible abilities. What you can do with heat and cold is absolutely astonishing!" and he beamed at Ninyani. "You are so very special for being born unique. In Teshon City, you will meet many other Shifts. The folk like you are a minority, but every one of your kind is unique!"

The boy's brow was furrowed; the words were difficult for him to accept. "I'm not a god?" he asked.

"I don't think so, my young friend," the mystic replied gently. "I believe you're part of that small group of people who just happened to be lucky enough to have been born with god-like gifts. That actually leads me nicely to the subject of my daughter, Lahari." He looked toward the door to the adjoining room, even though only Dozi was in it. "I know that you were very surprised to learn that the person you saw last night was actually a girl, *my* little girl, my little moth," he added in a voice full of adoration. "I know that when you saw her, she frightened you, and for that, I'm very sorry."

The mystic smiled at the boy. "However," he continued with a grin, "Lahari is also in fact a Shift, like you and Ilya, but her powers caused her body to change. She used to look like any other little girl.

Her hair was red; there were freckles on her cheeks. Then she changed, and I know you may have thought she was frightening, but I think my daughter is absolutely beautiful." The mystic's eyes were sparkling as he gushed about Lahari.

Dozi appeared at the door to the adjoining room. "I've got most of our stuff packed. Will you be ready to leave soon?" She did not wait for his reply. "I want to go down and find the others now and get them back here so we can leave as soon as possible. We've already lost half of the day."

"Ninyani and I will finish packing Theolan and my things while you find the others." He turned back to the boy as Dozi left. "I'm so sorry that you've lost so much, everything," the mystic said in a compassionate voice. "I know life will be very different, but will you come with us to Teshon City? There's nothing for you here in Bluewood, and I don't think you can go back home. I'm sorry," he said again.

Ninyani looked so small and frail. The boy was skinny and short, but the mystic knew that he was leaving childhood behind. The man felt sad for Ninyani, aside from the incalculable losses he suffered, he was also leaving behind the sweetness and innocence of youth. The mystic wondered what kind of person the boy would grow into.

"Please come with us," he reiterated.

Ninyani simply whispered, "Okay."

The mystic gave him a squeeze and said, "Let's finish up." Inside, the mystic was disappointed to be leaving Bluewood Village already. All he saw was the inn, but then he looked at Ninyani.

"You know," the mystic said with an expression of realization spreading across his face, "I think the whole purpose of us coming up here on this trip was to find you, Ninyani," and he did not feel so bad about leaving. He could not help but smile at the boy.

"Now, why don't you tell me a little bit more about yourself?" the mystic asked. "Do you have any hobbies? What do you like to do? Do you sing? Dance? Are you an artist, or a musician?"

The boy perked up at one of the words.

The mystic noticed and repeated himself. "Dance? Do you like to dance?"

Ninyani's eyes were wide and sparkling, but he shook his head *no*.

"You don't like to dance?" the mystic asked.

Ninyani blushed and replied, "I'm not allowed to dance."

"What do you mean? You were not allowed to dance?" The mystic scratched his chin.

"Boys don't dance in Frostflower. Only women and girls dance." Ninyani's voice became quieter, as he added, "I liked when they danced, and I wanted to dance with them."

The mystic grinned at the boy. "Oh-ho, I see," he said with a chuckle. "Girls! You like girls! And that's totally fine; you can like whomever you want to like."

"Their dancing is so pretty!"

The mystic was glad to have the boy talking about something with such enthusiasm, and he continued. "Do you like watching the girls dance?"

"*I* wanted to dance!" Ninyani declared.

"Well, let me tell you," the mystic said with a broad grin, "in Teshon City, anyone and everyone can dance! If you want to dance, I will find you someone who can teach those skills to you. In Teshon City," he continued in a dramatic tone, "you can dance in the streets, dance on the rooftops, dance in the markets, and dance all through the neighborhood where we live. I, for one, cannot *wait* to see you dance!"

The door to the adjoining suite opened. Theolan entered and joined his husband and Ninyani.

The four women stayed in the other room to pack.

"I'm sorry you didn't get to see anything, my love," Theolan said, as he kissed his husband. "Dozi told us what's going on, and that we need to go."

"We are already packing," the mystic replied with a smile. Hoping to keep the boy in a positive state of mind, he added, "Theolan, Ninyani is interested in taking dance lessons when we get back to the city. We need to find someone to teach him."

Theolan's face broke into a wide smile. "That sounds marvelous! Do you dance?" he asked the boy.

Ninyani shook his head *no* again.

"No?! Neither do I!" Theolan declared. He sounded delighted. "I've always wanted to learn how to dance. Shall we take dancing lessons together?"

Ninyani looked like he was about to burst into tears of joy.

Theolan stuck one leg out to the side and wiggled his hips, and Ninyani and the mystic giggled together at his silly performance.

"Turns out boys aren't supposed to dance in the village where Ninyani grew up," the mystic said to his husband, "but he's always enjoyed seeing others dance. It will be our mission this week to find him a dance instructor!"

"Not allowed to dance?!" Theolan scoffed. "All the more reason *to* dance!" He put a hand on the boy's shoulder.

Ninyani looked up at him and smiled.

"Hi, mystic," said Tchama, as she walked into the room. "What do you think of my new scarf?" She spun around.

He scrutinized the frilly pink and yellow material draped around Tchama's neck and grinned. "Why, it is quite lovely, my dear! A perfect selection." He noticed Ninyani's eyes were again wide and focused. He was staring at the scarf.

"That's Tchama," the mystic reminded him.

Ninyani ignored the man. "It's so pretty!" he exclaimed in a squeaky voice. "I..." he started. "It's just so pretty. I love it!"

Tchama looked between the mystic and his husband, and then back at the boy again. "Do you want it?" she offered. "You can have it, if you really like it."

Ninyani's eyes were like saucers, as if he was seeing the most beautiful thing in the world.

Tchama removed the scarf and extended it toward him.

"But that's a girl's clothes. I'm not supposed to wear girl clothes."

Ilya was in the doorway between the rooms and joined the conversation. "You can wear absolutely anything you want with us." She turned to Tchama. "That is so sweet of you to give it to him." Ilya smiled down at Ninyani. "Go ahead, take it. You're allowed to feel pretty."

The boy reached out a tentative hand, and he let out a quiet gasp, as Tchama handed him the scarf. "Wow," he whispered.

"Say *thank you*," the mystic urged with a smile.

Ninyani looked up at Ilya. She was a tall woman with broad shoulders and muscular arms. "Thank you," he said to her.

Ilya snorted a laugh. "I think he meant, to Tchama."

Ninyani shook his head, turned to Tchama, and repeated himself. "Thank you."

She reached out and helped him drape the scarf around his neck.

Dozi entered the room. "Almost ready to go?" she asked in a serious tone.

"Almost," the mystic responded, "and it turns out," he added, "our little Ninyani here knows several methods of dealing with Bluewood's icewyrm problem. There doesn't happen to be an icewyrm skeleton lying around somewhere, is there?"

Dozi looked confused. "I always thought those things were indestructible. You can kill them?"

"Only with their own bones, apparently," the mystic informed her.

"Helpful, but also unhelpful." Dozi shrugged.

Lahari called out from the other room. "Ada!" and her father joined her. She pulled him over to the side and whispered, "Someone clocked me at the market."

"What do you mean?" he asked in concern. "Someone realized that you're a Bio-Shift?"

"I didn't notice that my scarf slipped off part of my cheek," she explained, "and one of the vendors asked me what was wrong with my skin. So I agree with Dozi; I'd also be happy to leave immediately. There's something about this village that's even less welcoming than some of the areas in Teshon City. It was a mistake coming here."

Her father nodded. "I think we came here for the boy," he replied. "As much as I don't want to immediately make the three-day journey back down right after arriving, I think we were just supposed to find him, to find him and leave. We've already packed," he added.

Dozi stuck her head into the room and said, "Let's get the fuck out of here."✪

Chapter 11 – Vion, Part Three

As the evening's early winter sunset began to steal the light from Teshon City, the Principal Messiah was with Vion and his two lieutenants in front of the west dormitory. They huddled together in the glow of a single lamp, surrounded by the oncoming darkness.

"Since the bodies inside," the Principal Messiah declared, "are in the same three horrible conditions as the other murder scene, I presume we are dealing with a trio of very powerful Shifts who are going around and murdering our brethren without cause."

Vion kept his cynical snicker to himself. In his mind, the *cause* for these Shifts' actions was not up for debate. He would not have hesitated to murder every single Shift in Teshon City, and he could understand that some of them might have similar feelings toward Messiahs, but he did not interrupt his superior.

"You three will spend the night examining the crime scene while it's fresh, but an example needs to be made," the woman continued, "and it needs to be made in Gate Town. I will not stand to have our authority questioned or resisted, nor will I be satisfied until we have access to every part of the city and each inhabitant. No angry mob will stop us."

She pointed at Vion and the two inquisitors. "You, my holy Truth Seekers, will go find where these murderous Shifts are hiding, and if you cannot bring them to face my judgment, I expect you to end them outright."

"It shall be done, milady," Vion replied.

The Principal Messiah smiled. "Tomorrow night, you three will rein vengeance on our sworn enemies."★

Chapter 12 – Messiah Temple

"We're going back out tonight," S'Kay declared as she slipped over the concrete barrier with Gawa and Eroli. They dropped down to the old Oselian airfield, ducked past the caution signs, and entered their underground hideout.

The sun was yet to rise.

"No, we can't," Eroli retorted. "It's too soon."

"I don't know what your resistance is," S'Kay said with a frown, "but hear me out, because I refuse to stop. I want to kill as many cannibals as we can, and I think we need to do it sooner rather than later. What we just did will lead to some sort of retaliation." She lit a candle. "I'm surprised nothing came of our first attack. We've experienced two great successes, but I suspect that from now on the other two Messiah houses will be heavily guarded and under surveillance. However, I have something else in mind."

"Really, what?" Gawa asked. Eroli may have been apprehensive, but Gawa was excited.

"I think we need to bring death to their doorstep," S'Kay replied.

"What do you mean?" Gawa asked, but Eroli gasped.

S'Kay smiled at his reaction, and she brushed her fingers over the feathers that grew from her arms. "So, you understand my intention," she said to him.

"*What?*" Gawa repeated.

"We won't need Tualu for this one," S'Kay informed her. "Now that the doors can no longer close, there are always guards stationed at them. We are going to kill them and leave their bodies in the street."

Gawa looked both amazed and surprised. "*Yes,*" she whispered, and she turned to Eroli, "S'Kay is right; we can't stop what we've started."

Eroli ran his claws through his thick fur in a nervous manner. "Our actions are going to lead to confrontation," he said.

"It's about bleeding time for some of our kin to step up and take action," S'Kay responded. She looked out of the entrance. The night's darkness still clutched the city. "Dawn is not far. Meet me at Red Raven's pub this evening, after sundown."

Gawa said, "I'll be there," and Eroli reluctantly nodded his agreement.

The three left their hideout and returned to the city, and the sun soon spread its light over the world. The rest of that day dragged for them.

S'Kay and Gawa were ready for the night's coming slaughter, and evening could not arrive fast enough, but Eroli was fearful.

When sunset finally dimmed the world, he made his way to one of the few taverns that catered to Biological Shifts in Shifton. Eroli took a deep breath before he pulled open the door to Red Raven's.

Gawa was already waiting inside.

He approached. "I don't know about this," he said to her.

"Don't talk about it," she replied sternly. "S'Kay will be here in a moment."

"I don't know…" Eroli started to say, but from behind him, S'Kay's voice interrupted.

"You don't have to come." Her words sounded icy. "Gawa and I can do it by ourselves." She handed Eroli and Gawa each a folded cloak.

Without sitting to join them or speaking another word, S'Kay turned and walked to the door of the tavern.

Gawa rose and followed her.

Eroli grabbed his glass, knocked back the rest of his beverage, and jogged behind the two women.

S'Kay draped herself with a heavy hooded cloak, and the other two wrapped themselves in the garments she provided them. The early winter night quickly grew dark, and the three made their way down narrow corridors until they were through the neighborhood and out of Gate Town.

The Messiah Tower's silhouette loomed against the night sky. A moment later, the trio was hidden in a shadowy alleyway around the corner from the temple. S'Kay peeked out, then she pulled her head back.

"I can only see two guards," she informed Gawa and Eroli. "I don't know if there's anyone else farther around the tower, but the two of them are just standing there."

"Are they armed?" Eroli asked.

"They're Messiahs," Gawa answered, "so it doesn't matter if they're armed. We need to take them out before they can react to us."

"It would be convenient if one of us possessed a ranged ability," Eroli complained, "but all three of us need to be right on top of our targets."

S'Kay ignored his comment. "Head through that building," she ordered, and she pointed. "You should be able to get closest to the guard who's closest to the door by going through there. Gawa, you head down into that runoff ditch and creep all the way until you are beneath the other. Once you're both in position, I'll approach from the front and draw their focus." S'Kay dropped her heavy cloak and ruffled her feathers. "You need to strike the instant I've distracted them. We're here to take out Messiahs; I don't want them killing me."

She waited as Gawa and Eroli moved into their positions, then she stepped out into the street. The unique woman with a bird-like appearance began to approach the dilapidated front of the Messiah temple, and she immediately caught the men's attention.

"Hey!" one of them yelled, but his words were cut off, as he and his fellow guard suddenly found themselves at the mercy of Gawa and Eroli.

Both Messiahs tried to scream, but all that came from them were wheezing and gurgling noises as they died. Eroli's victim hit the ground as a crystalline shell of himself and shattered into countless glittering fragments. Gawa's purple electricity caused the other man to go rigid where he stood. In an instant, he was nothing more than a scorched corpse that fell to the pavement.

"*What the fuck?!*" barked a voice behind Gawa, and another pair of Messiahs came around from the far side of the Tower.

They froze in shocked horror, but it only took a moment for them to compose themselves. Both reached for the clubs that hung from their belts.

Gawa was closest, and before they could attack, she screamed and lunged forward. She grabbed both men and poured her devastating cosmic powers into them. Their limbs went rigid as they burned to cinders, and their charred bodies crashed to the street. They crackled with tiny bolts of violet lightning.

"Let's get out of here, now!" snapped Eroli.

"Agreed, that's four public bodies for them to deal with," S'Kay said. "Gawa, let's move," and the three were off again down an alley, into the darkness✪

Chapter 13 – Journey Home

With the winter sun already at its zenith, Dozi and the group from Teshon City, with the addition of Ninyani, turned their backs on Bluewood Village. They started the long journey south along the Pinewood path. The mountain air was cold, but there was no wind blowing against the travelers.

Ninyani left his home in Frostflower without any possessions, save for the clothes on his back, but he did not require anything extra for the trip. His garments from the far north were more than sufficient against the weather, and Tchama's frilly pink and yellow scarf was still around his neck. It was a lovely accent to his furs.

Over the long days of their trek back to the city, Ninyani complimented each of the four women on different articles of their clothing, and they all shared things with him. Dozi's rainbow-striped knit cap with a flower pin caught his eye, and she let him wear it, happily accepting his thick fur hat in exchange. He was also enamored by Lahari's periwinkle blue mittens, and she gave them to him. She borrowed an extra pair of gloves from her father.

Those initial fears that Ninyani felt at seeing Lahari's physical appearance were replaced with a sense of wonder. She did not mind his probing questions about her unique body, and she answered everything he asked about her quills and her yellow eyes and her scaly blue skin. He learned about the black hole of energy that dwelt inside her, and the ways its power had affected the different types of people who threatened or challenged her.

Ninyani spent part of the long days walking beside and talking with each member of the group. The mystic told him much about life in Teshon City, and he offered the boy a place to stay with him and his husband and daughter. He described the neighborhoods and different groups of people who made up the inhabitants of the city. The mystic also enthusiastically answered any questions Ninyani asked.

While Theolan walked beside the boy, he talked quite a lot about food. He told him of the produce markets and seasonal fairs. He went into detail about the plethora of snacks and treats at them, and also the live entertainment. Theolan described the singers, dancers, and sometimes even Shifts who would display their powers at the celebrations.

Ninyani was riveted by the details.

None of the Shifts, Ilya, Lahari, or Ninyani used their powers during the journey south. They explained to him the dangers of using his abilities in public, and that revealing he was a Shift would make him a target. They let him know that only in certain places was it safe for Shifts to show their abilities, and only ever among their own kind or with others who were accepting.

The boy had used his powers very few times, and *not* using them was easy for him.

Of the group, Tchama spent the most time walking beside Ninyani. The two of them developed a rapport that warmed the mystic's heart. The way Tchama and Ninyani laughed and joked together was like she was his big sister.

The pair discussed everything from fishing in the harbor waters around Teshon City, to how Ilya was gone some of the time on her trips into the mountains, and also about where each of their group lived in relation to everyone else. The two talked about Ninyani's life in Frostflower, his chores, the other children, even the cruel old Shift who thought he was a god and lived among his worshipers. Ninyani avoided the topic of his mother.

While they walked, Tchama made jokes about the way her messy hair looked, and Ninyani giggled at how different her accent sounded from his. He taught her a song that the Frostflower children used to sing together, and Tchama promised to take him to every single one of the Shift cafés in Gate Town and Shifton.

At one point, the two of them burst out laughing, when a whole group of chubby little chipmunks scampered across the path in front of them. The awkward critters panicked and disappeared back into the underbrush with frantic waddling steps.

Ninyani spent time getting to know everyone else, but the bond between him and Tchama was instantaneous. They even held hands for much of the journey.

On the third morning, the sun came out and warmed the travelers.

Ilya unbuttoned her jacket, and Ninyani's eyes sparkled at the sight of the sweater that she was wearing underneath.

By the time the group finally arrived in Teshon City, quite a few of Ninyani's heavy furs were replaced by the four women's more colorful garments, and there was a lightness in the boy's step. Despite the horrors he experienced in his village, over the several days of travel, he spent very little of his time in a state of misery. The mystic knew that someday Ninyani would need to deal with what he went through, but he saw a resilience in the boy that gave him hope.

The group was kind and generous to Ninyani, and he could not help but feel drawn to the people who had saved him from the devastation of Frostflower. There were moments when his mother's bloated and rotting corpse flashed into his mind and brought him to tears, but the comfort he received from Tchama in particular was like a balm to the child's broken soul.

It was the middle of the afternoon on their fourth day of walking when they led Ninyani through the old Oselian gates, and the group entered Shifton. A few minutes later they were at the house where the mystic, Theolan, and Lahari all lived together.

Dozi nudged Tchama and Ilya, and she nodded her head toward their basement home.

Tchama knelt down in front of Ninyani and asked him, "Will you be okay here?"

He looked up at the mystic and Theolan who both smiled at him with encouragement. "I'd like to stay," Ninyani replied to Tchama,

She wrapped her arms around his little frame. "I think we three are going to head home," she informed him. "Dozi and Ilya and I live just a little farther into the city, in an area called the Spritehood. The mystic and Theolan used to live near our place. Anyway," she continued, "all of us have had a *long* several days, so why don't you get settled here with them, and we will come see how you're doing tomorrow?"

Everyone said their goodbyes and Dozi, Ilya, and Tchama began the last little leg of their journey together.

When they were right around the corner from the secret basement that the three of them called home, Tchama stopped walking. "Wait a second," she said, "let's pop over to Auntie Peg's place and tell her about Ninyani. I think he's really going to like her."

"They should definitely meet," Ilya agreed.

"Why don't we wait till morning?" Dozi suggested.

"It's two blocks away," Tchama whined.

Dozi rolled her eyes and said, "Fine! Let's go see her."

Rounding a few blocks led them to the front of Peggy's Potions. The door was locked; a note informed them why.

Sorry for the inconvenience, but the shop is closed right now. Please come back again soon, or if you need me immediately, I am at the Sunwood clinic at the corner of Harbor Ave. and Teshon Blvd. Have a great day!

"Okay, let's head home," Dozi declared.

"Shouldn't we go to the clinic?" Tchama recommended, but Ilya replied.

"I've been close enough to the blood corruption," she said, "and haven't you? I could really do without seeing the patients who are suffering from it."

"We are all exhausted," Dozi added. "Why don't we go home and get clean, maybe even have a bath, and then, if you still want to go find Auntie Peg, we can talk about it afterward. But I'm hungry. I stink. I would love to be home after this crazy whirlwind vacation we just went on. What was it, a week? Eight days? I've lost track."

"Dozi's right," Ilya agreed, and Tchama conceded.

Several minutes later, they slipped behind the old fan cage and ducked into the hidden entrance of the basement.

"Turn on the boiler," Dozi instructed Tchama. "I'll get the tap, and Ilya, will you start spreading out our travel clothes so that they air out before we wash them?"

"A bath is going to feel so magical after all that hiking," Tchama replied, as she got on her hands and knees and reached under the huge metal barrel they used as a bathtub. She cranked on the flame.

Dozi walked over to the wall and turned on the faucet. The water only came out cold, but she always appreciated that running water was accessible in her basement.

During the previous summer, when Tchama was welcomed to move in with Dozi and Ilya, she devised a way for the three of them to enjoy hot baths. She knew of several old metal barrels that were coated in a protective sealant developed by the Oselians. The trio managed to get one onto a wheeled cart, and they rolled the barrel back to their home. It almost did not fit through the hidden door, and getting it down the stairs was precarious, but their giant bathtub quickly became a treasured part of their home.

After Dozi first moved into the secret cellar, she tapped into an old natural gas line and fashioned a makeshift stove. She repeated the process and ran more tubing along the wall to the space under the giant barrel.

Ilya turned out to be a talented woodworker, and she built a base for the bottom of the inside of the barrel that supported three wooden lounge chairs and a footrest, all of which she also built from scratch. The base and footrest kept their feet off the primary heat source underneath the tub. She also carved three small paddles, and the women used them to circulate the hotter water up from the bottom.

Their first few baths ended up getting too hot, and Dozi added a shutoff valve for the gas that they could reach without getting out of the tub. She also happened to have in her possession an old thermometer that she found in an Oselian warehouse by the Stone Wharf. Even though the tub took a little while to fill and heat, the bath was worth it every time.

Dozi grabbed a meat pie for each of them, and they ate with the quiet sound of the splashing water. They were all exhausted from the journey.

When they finished eating, the three women peeled off their heavy outer layers and helped Ilya spread out the rest of their rank clothes. She often came back from her trips into the mountains with fresh herbs, and the trio regularly made cleansing rinses from them. They spritzed their garments and wiped down the dirtiest and smelliest parts of their bodies before the bath was full.

After a little while, the water was at a nice warm temperature, and they climbed over the lip of the tub. The three always sat in the same chairs. They often talked and laughed, sharing the details of their days and discussing the markets where Dozi sold her mushrooms. However, that night, the silence lingered, only punctuated by quiet sighs of contentment from each of them.

Eventually, the water was hot enough that they turned off the flame, and the three sat soaking for quite a while. It soothed their muscles and purified their bodies.

One by one, as each was ready, they climbed back out of the tub. They dried themselves and dressed in their sleep clothes, and even though it was still early evening, the three were soon asleep.

Up the stairs, outside their basement home, the quiet city streets were suddenly filled with the ringing of the Teshon City warning bells★

Chapter 14 – Vion, Part Four

Vion and his two inquisitors rushed through the dark city streets of the industrial district. The Principal Messiah sent word for the trio to hold their attack and report to the temple at once, but as they turned the corner that led to the Messiah Tower, they were surprised to see a crowd in front of it. Several heavily armed guards blocked the way, but they nodded Vion and his officers through the perimeter. They saw the Principal Messiah kneeling beside four more corpses.

"Curse these monsters!" she raged. "Now they've attacked our sacred place!" The Principal Messiah stood upright as Vion approached. "Our fallen kin at this attack site," she informed him, "only display two of the three types of murderous energies we've encountered. With any luck, our enemies are facing dissension in their ranks. Come inside, now," she commanded, and without waiting, she stormed in through the broken doors.

Vion left his inquisitors in the street and followed her.

"Do you know what happens when a Messiah consumes a second mantis gland?" the Principal Messiah asked.

"A second, milady?"

She furrowed her brow. "Yes, *a second*," she replied. The woman glared at Vion with an expression that dared him to interrupt her again. "You remember eating the mantis gland that turned you into a Messiah, correct?" Her question was rhetorical, and her tone was sarcastic. She continued without allowing him to reply.

"Far to the south, the mountains end in a vast flatland, but between the two is a region of foothills that serves as the monsterdom of the mutated. Those twisted addicts," she continued, as she began to climb the stairs, "are not part of this society."

Vion followed.

"Their kind are not welcome in Teshon City," the Principal Messiah elucidated, "but from time to time, my brother comes to visit."

She reached the top step, approached a window, and pointed down.

Vion joined her and looked where she indicated.

In a narrow alleyway adjacent to the tower, a coachman stepped down from his carriage and opened its door. Vion was shocked by what he saw.

Something vaguely humanoid emerged from the Tower at street level. The creature was naked, with the same skin tone as the Principle Messiah. However, unlike her, this being was made up of too much *person*. Its arms were normal human arms, as were its legs, but there were too many of each. The thing slithered into the carriage, moving more like an animal than a human, and the coachman shut the door behind it.

"*What on earth was that?*" Vion exclaimed.

"That's my brother," the Principal Messiah replied in a calm tone. "After his second mantis gland, he grew the arm that comes out of his sternum. You couldn't see it from here, but his mouth also developed..." she paused, "another mouth, for lack of a better explanation. It's almost as if he has two separate lower jaws."

She continued. "The third and fourth mantis glands he ate grew him extra legs and the fleshy boulder that protrudes from his back. There are also fingers that extend out all over his upper chest, and he has a partial arm sticking out from one side that just pokes like an elbow. His fifth mantis gland gave him a third eye on the back of his head, a second penis, and also a foot coming out of one shoulder blade."

Vion watched the carriage until it rolled into the main street and disappeared from sight.

"He will never be the same again," the Principal Messiah went on, "and he will likely never stop hunting for mantis glands. Don't worry," she answered before Vion could even formulate the question, "he always asks, but never gets any from us when he visits me. No," she added, "in fact, let me show you the way that we, your superiors, enjoy Shift."

The Principal Messiah continued up the stairs to the next story and Vion followed her. She nodded at a pair of guards who stood in front of a massive steel door, and one of them opened it. Vion followed her into a dark room with one of the guards behind him, and the man closed the door again. Vion heard a harsh snicker from the Principal Messiah.

She flipped a switch and the lights flickered on, but Vion could not comprehend what he saw.

Strapped to a gurney was a man. He was covered in a sheet up to his neck, and many tubes connected him to several different pieces of equipment. They appeared medical in nature to Vion's untrained eye.

"Bring me two SF teas," the Principal Messiah commanded of the guard.

On a cart in one corner, the man set a kettle to boil on a heating element, and he collected two teacups from the shelf on the wall above it. The guard approached the largest piece of equipment, held one of the mugs under a tiny spigot on the machine, and he pulled its tap. A few drops of clear watery fluid dripped into one cup, and he swapped it for the other, then turned off the little faucet. A moment later the kettle was steaming and the man poured some warm water into the mugs. He handed one to each of them, nodded, and exited the room.

The Principal Messiah took a sip.

"Drink," she commanded Vion.

"What is it?" he asked her.

She made a smug face and took another sip.

He looked down at his mug. It appeared to contain only water, and he tried it. It tasted of nothing. He sniffed it and took another sip.

"I don't taste anything. What does *SF* stand for?"

"Spinal fluid," she replied casually. "They want to call us cannibals, we'll act like cannibals."

Vion looked down at his mug with a disgusted expression.

"*Keep your judgments to yourself,*" the Principal Messiah snapped. Her scowl was back in place. "Don't pretend that you haven't eaten part of a Shift."

Vion looked up at her and quietly asked in a kowtowed voice, "What does drinking Shift spinal fluid do?"

"It is power over the powerful," she replied with a wicked laugh. "I would eat every scrap of this monstrosity," and the woman waved at the helpless victim, "except for his mantis gland. I have no interest in mutating like my brother. This *thing,*" she spat at the unconscious man, "is meat. He is prey to our kind. He is nothing more than an animal upon which we feed." The Principal Messiah finished her beverage and placed the mug on a table.

She looked at Vion expectantly, as he took another sip and then also finished his beverage. "Come with me," she commanded.

They descended and returned to the dark street in front of the damaged doors.

A small army of Messiahs was guarding the base of the Temple.

"I want you lot," the Principal Messiah ordered, and she waved at a group of them who were huddled together, "to join Vion on a mission of vengeance tonight. Bring battle to the filth that live in Gate Town." She nodded at Vion and returned to the interior of the tower.

He looked up at the night sky and told them all, "When the buildings are burning, there will be plenty of light by which to fight."

The moon was beginning to slide up from the horizon, as he and his inquisitors led the march. Darkness would not stop Vion from accomplishing the task that his leader set before him. At the edge of Gate Town, he ordered the Messiahs to diverge. They began to head down several different narrow streets, and soon there was an ominous orange glow on the underside of the thin clouds above.

Gate Town was on fire.

Screams rang out from a number of different directions around the neighborhood, as the inhabitants realized that something was terribly wrong.

Vion and Proge stalked down a quiet street with Chenchi.

A fleeing man ran out and tried to get past her, but she grabbed him by the head and asked in a booming voice, *"Where are the murderers?"* Chenchi simultaneously smashed his skull against the wall, making her question moot.

Proge circumvented his fellow Messiah and lunged for another confused and frightened man who stepped outside to see what was happening.

However, the individual turned out to be a Shift, and he released an orb of energy that appeared to collide with Proge. The sphere of power passed through the Messiah as if he were nothing; at the same time, it also absorbed part of him. The ball of light then vanished, and one of Proge's entire arms and a massive portion of his torso disappeared with it. He fell to the pavement, but he was dead before he hit the ground.

Chenchi grabbed a cinder block from the alleyway floor and hurtled it at the Shift man. Her aim was off and it exploded against the wall. He launched another orb of power, but Chenchi dove out of the way. She snatched up a pipe, threw it like a spear, and her aim was true. It impaled the man through his guts and nailed him to the wall behind. He feebly clutched at the horrible metal tube that protruded from his stomach, but he managed to launch another orb. It was much smaller and shot wide, hitting the side of a building and taking a chunk of bricks and mortar with it.

Chenchi roared as she charged the man, wielding another cinder block like it was a club. She spun her body and swung the concrete brick in a majestic arc through the air, held fast in her empowered grip. The Messiah slammed her makeshift weapon into the skewered man's head and it exploded with a halo of brains on the wall around it.

"Fucking Shift," Chenchi spat.

"You better find the mantis gland in all that mess," Vion warned her. "I want it."

He knelt beside Proge's body and examined the damage. "This doesn't match the three types of corpses that we've found at the massacre sites. That Shift was not one of our targets," he declared. "The killers are still out there."

Chenchi was not paying attention to Vion's observations, and she stormed around the corner into a startled group of two men and a woman. There was no resistance from the three.

She body-checked one man into a building so hard that the wall cracked and he fell to the ground. Blood seeped from his ears and mouth. Chenchi uppercutted the woman in the jaw, snapping her head back and breaking her neck instantly. Her corpse crashed to the pavement. The third man tried to run, but Chenchi grabbed his wrist. She brought her opposite hand to his ribs, and with horrible screams from both Chenchi and her victim, she ripped off his arm. The man was silenced, as she pummeled him with his own limb. She left him a bloody mess.

Vion stood at the corner and smiled at Chenchi's carnage. A man suddenly exited a building between them, and Vion charged at him. He swung his empowered fist like a wrecking ball and it collided with the man's jaw. Vion expected his head to twist around, but the man barely flinched.

Without warning, the would-be victim struck out, punching Vion in the guts with a battering ram fist. The man landed several blows before Chenchi grabbed him from behind. Vion retaliated and the two Messiahs forced the man to the ground.

"Traitor!" Chenchi screamed. "You fucking traitor!" She pushed his face against the pavement. "You're disgusting! A Messiah, living with Shifts? You are a predator and they are your fucking food, and you will die a traitor's death!"

The two Messiahs would have struggled to kill one of their own nigh-invulnerable kind, and the ex-Messiah man seemed more irritated by them than worried, but Vion pulled a diamond dagger from its sheath at his hip.

"The Principal Messiah stole this from the High Chemist," he said, "and she entrusted it to me."

The pinned man's eyes went wild with fear. It took a lot to frighten the empowered, but the blade could easily end his life, and he tried to scream.

Vion stabbed the man in his jugular, yanked the knife out, and slashed it across his throat. He and Chenchi stepped back, as the man squirmed on the pavement and gripped at his neck. His mouth gaped like a fish, but only gurgling noises came out of it. Chenchi approached and put her foot on his chest. She held him against the concrete as his blood flowed and his eyes became unfocused. He groped feebly at her ankle, then he fell still in a pool of his own blood.

"Fucking traitor," Vion growled. "Set that building on fire," he ordered Chenchi, and he pointed at a wooden structure.

People in the streets all around them screamed and fled from the violence. Many were hunted down.

Vion shook off the pummeling he took, rounded a corner, and he collided with a group of angry men.

They were armed with clubs and bludgeons, and they swung at him with their weapons.

After facing off against someone as an ex-Messiah who was as strong as himself, Vion threw his hands up in defense, but he was barely aware of the blows. The men were all mere humans.

Vion turned a wicked smile at them and lashed out with both fists. One of them hit so hard that Vion's hand entered a man's guts. He gripped a fistful of organs and yanked his hand out again. The man collapsed beside the pile of his innards. Vion's other brick of knuckles smashed into the side of a man's lower jaw and it was torn completely from his head. His throat was ripped open by the terrible impact, and he collapsed, convulsing to the pavement and clutching at the chasm that was now his face.

Vion bore down on the others, slamming one into and straight through a brick wall, breaking countless of the man's bones. Another caught a downward blow of Vion's fist to his collarbone, and the man crumpled with his spine bent to a horrible angle.

Something slammed into the back of Vion's head, but it felt like no more than a gentle tap.

A man was holding an iron fire poker that now was warped and bent near the end where it came into contact with Vion's almost indestructible skull.

Vion grabbed the man, squatted down, and he leapt straight up with all his might. The two of them launched high into the air above the Teshon City streets.

"Look down," Vion said when they were at the apex, and he let the man go.

Both of them fell, tumbling through the air with the concrete speeding up from below, and all the while Vion laughed. His terrible laughter rang out through the city streets, and he continued to laugh, as both he and the man with the fire poker hit the ground.

Vion kept right on cackling, as he lay in the crater that his body created when he landed in the pavement. The man had impacted beside him, but his body made no effect whatsoever on the concrete.

He was mangled and twisted. Both his arms were pierced at multiple locations where his broken bones protruded through the flesh. One leg was under him facing the wrong direction, and his other was in pieces; his foot was no longer connected, and the shin only remained attached to the knee by a gruesome chunk of tendony flesh. The man wheezed the last of his breaths beneath the sound of Vion's laughter.

Chenchi stepped up and reached down to Vion. She assisted him to his feet and brushed him off rather roughly with a smirk.

"That was a good kill," she said to him.

Vion grinned. "We're done here. Did you get that mantis gland?"

Chenchi answered him with a villainous smile and patted her hip pouch.

Vion nodded, pulled a whistle from his pocket, and blew a long shrill note. He took a breath and blew another. Vion let out several piercing shrieks with the whistle, then he nodded at Chenchi.

As they returned the way they came, Vion's eyes moved over the corpse of Proge. They left his body in the street and made their way out of the neighborhood. At the edge of Gate Town, Vion blew the whistle several more times, and the other officers who were assigned to him by the Principal Messiah also abandoned their assault. Several were covered in blood. Two others of the group along with Proge did not return.

Vion and his horde turned their backs on the burning neighborhood and left the chaos behind.

All along the border to Gate Town, the fires continued to burn✪

Chapter 15 – Confronting Devastation

The winter dawn began to illuminate through a gap in the clouds on the eastern horizon. Its light shimmered across the sea. The rest of the sky was overcast.

Gawa, Eroli, and S'Kay made their way along dark alleys and kept to the shadows where they could. The heavy cloaks they wore helped conceal each of their unique appearances and prevented them from attracting attention to themselves. They approached the entrance to Gate Town, rounded a corner, and were startled to see an ominous orange glow on the underside of the clouds above the neighborhood. The trio drew closer, and they saw the flames.

"This is our fault," Eroli declared.

"None of us," S'Kay spat, "will be taking credit or blame for the actions of Messiahs. There was never any question that what we are doing would result in consequences. We could not have known what the Messiahs would do, but you can't tell me that you didn't anticipate violence."

"The worse they are," Gawa added, "the more likely people will join our cause."

"But I thought you said that we won't be adding anyone else to our group." Eroli looked at them both, appalled. "We're not doing this again, are we?"

They approached a group of people who were trying to put out the flames of a burning building.

"We absolutely are," S'Kay replied under her breath. "We've taken out 27 Messiahs, but through all time, how many of *our* kind have been slaughtered? And now, they've retaliated against civilians who were not involved. The Messiahs have made themselves the enemies of Teshon City."

"We need to strike again," Gawa concurred.

S'Kay ruffled her feathers. "I've got another idea of what to attack."

"What, not *who*?" Gawa asked.

They approached several more people who were standing next to a row of sheet-covered bundles that were stretched out on the pavement.

"Those are bodies," Eroli whispered, as they passed.

"Of course they're bodies," S'Kay responded.

"Each one of those people're dead because of us."

S'Kay stopped walking, pushed Eroli up against a wall, and grabbed him by the cloak. "Keep it together," she growled. "The Messiahs have their own corpses they're dealing with, but if you're feeling guilty, why don't you help one of these groups with the fires or with the injured."

A voice rang out on a side street, and the three looked in its direction.

"If anyone would like to volunteer for our new neighborhood watch, please come and sign up at the podium."

"You can join them," S'Kay said to Eroli, "but make no mistake, this is war, and this is only the beginning."

The three of them turned down a side street.

"Sunset tonight, in the underground," S'Kay stated to them.

"No, it's too soon," Eroli retorted. "The Messiahs will be on high alert."

S'Kay simply repeated herself. "Sunset, tonight, the underground."

"I'm in," Gawa declared.

Eroli gave the two women an uncertain nod★

Chapter 16 – Dozi & Ilya

As the rising sun glittered on the ocean, Dozi made her way with Ilya and Tchama into Gate Town. The city's emergency bells rang for over an hour, and now it was quiet. Entering the neighborhood to the sounds of crackling fires was eerie. A few structures were still smoking but no longer in flames, and a group of people was almost in control of another burning building.

Down a side street, the three women heard a voice call out to a gathered crowd. A woman was standing at a podium.

"Gate Town needs protection, and I propose that we organize defensive squads to patrol the perimeter, and in particular, the border to Shifton."

Dozi, Ilya, and Tchama stopped to listen.

"We are here to establish the first neighborhood watch," the woman continued.

Tchama pulled Dozi and Ilya's jacket sleeves and said in a whiny voice, "I really want to check up on Ninyani."

"Go ahead," Dozi replied.

"Yeah, we can meet you at home later," Ilya added.

Tchama ran off toward the mystic's house, and the woman at the podium continued.

"I know that some of you are ex-Messiahs, and if any of you are willing to volunteer, we could use your strength along the border. A group of mostly Shifts and Bio-Shifts should make up the squads that patrol the entrance to Shifton, but whoever else wants to join is welcome. If anyone would like to volunteer for our new neighborhood watch, please come and sign up at the podium."

The woman kept speaking, but Dozi turned to Ilya and said, "I'm joining."

Ilya looked both surprised and impressed. "Really?" she asked. "Do I sense a little of Agrell's nobility coming out in you?"

Dozi rolled her eyes. "Are you coming, too, or what?"

"Oh, you know I'll join," Ilya replied.

They stepped up and added their names to the growing list.

The woman at the podium began directing people. "We need help putting out fires and assisting with the injured during the day, and tonight we will need patrols for the streets."

Dozi and Ilya spent the morning helping however they could. When they were hungry, they stopped by the mystic's house, and he was thrilled to make them lunch before sending them back out to do their part.

Tchama remained with Ninyani.

Dozi and Ilya stayed in Gate Town the rest of the day, helping the residents of the devastated neighborhood. At sundown, it turned out that several chefs worked together to prepare a large dinner for all the volunteers, and everyone ate enthusiastically.

It was late in the evening when Dozi and Ilya finally returned home. They filled the tub and enjoyed a long, hot soak. Each ate a meat pie, and they were unconscious the moment their heads hit their pillows.

Both of them slept through a terrible crash that came from the other side of the Spritehood✪

Chapter 17 – Auntie Peg

The winter sun was already ducking behind the jagged horizon of the inland mountains, when Auntie Peg heard a knock on the door at the front of her shop. She often locked up early during the shorter days of the cold season, and there was an event in the evening that she was looking forward to attending. She stepped out from behind her counter, and she saw Tchama's smiling face through the window.

Auntie Peg opened the door and the young woman asked, "What does *all secondhand* mean?"

Below the sign for Peggy's Potions, those two words were painted in yellow.

"*All secondhand* means," Auntie Peg explained, "I purchase the potion-making products in my shop for a considerable discount, because I get them from other healers or mystics who are going out of business, or shops that have already closed. Down the street, a Demifae man died this week, and I've got six boxes of his unused ingredients in the back. I will be putting them out on display around the shop over the next day or two."

Auntie Peg continued. "What *all secondhand* means is that no Shift died by my actions in order to procure all of these really quite miraculous ingredients we use these days for healing. Unfortunately, it's true that everything in my shop has been charmed by a mantis gland at some point or other," she explained, "but all of these ingredients would have just been thrown away, and they are still very beneficial to us. So I collect them and try to make sure the life of the Shift that was lost in order to create these magical ingredients, was not in vain. Now," Auntie Peg concluded, "what can I do for you this evening, my dear?"

Tchama was beaming as she stepped through the door and closed it behind her. "You have to meet Ninyani! He's staying with Lahari and her dads."

"Well, that's very exciting," Auntie Peg replied. "I look forward to meeting him someday. Is there something else you need from me right now? I'm headed out to a fundraiser, and I'd really like to get there early."

"Yeah, okay, erm..." Tchama said, furrowing her brow in concern, "I don't mean to assume, but I wanted to tell you; I think Ninyani is like you."

Auntie Peg looked intrigued. "Tell me more."

"I guess the long and short of it..." Tchama stumbled over her words, "is, erm, I mean, so..." She paused and gathered her thoughts. "Okay, a bunch of us traveled north to Bluewood, and Ilya saw smoke on the horizon, so she flew to it and found Ninyani. He's just a young boy, but he ended up borrowing a bunch of clothes, in particular from us girls."

"How marvelous!" Auntie Peg declared. "I know something about being a boy who likes girls' clothes," she said with a grin. Then she paused and gave Tchama a contemplative look. "Actually, were you hoping I would meet him now? He might really enjoy and benefit from going to the show with me tonight, and you are more than welcome to join me, as well."

Auntie Peg continued in a pleasant tone. "Also, I understand why you are excited for me to meet him, but it's not really someone else's place to make declarations about another person's feelings and experiences. Especially since he's young, this may be the first time he has experimented. I am excited to meet him, and I look forward to getting to know the person he grows into."

Tchama looked appalled. "I didn't mean to tell you any of his secrets!"

Auntie Peg interrupted her. "No, no, it's okay. This type of thing is a learning experience," she explained. "You will meet people in the future who seem a certain way to you, but your perception may not be congruent with how they see themselves, or who they are on the inside. It's very normal for us to assume and make judgments about other people. What's difficult," Auntie Peg said, smiling at Tchama and putting her very large hand on the young woman's shoulder, "is *not* assuming, allowing people to open up on their own."

"I'm sorry," Tchama said in a pleading tone.

"My dear," Auntie Peg replied in a calm voice, "you have nothing about which to be sorry. Why don't you lead the way and bring me to him? And please, tell me his name again."

"Ninyani," Tchama replied. "Oh yeah," she added, "and I really, *really* don't mean to out him in a different way, but I think it's important you know that he's a Shift."

"Ah, it makes sense that he's staying in Shifton with the boys." She waved her hand toward the door to her shop. "I wouldn't be surprised if the mystic wants to join us tonight at the event, as well," Auntie Peg added. "Shall we head out?"

The two exited and locked the shop behind them. Before long they were passing under the shadow of the Messiah temple, and after several more blocks, they reached the entrance to Gate Town.

"The venue is not far down that street," Auntie Peg commented. She pointed at a crossroad as they passed it.

"What's the fundraiser for?" Tchama asked.

"The hosts are trying to raise money in support of the people who were most hurt by the attack on Gate Town. They are also trying to bolster peoples' spirits." Auntie Peg sighed. "Last I heard, the death toll from the attack was up to 37, and who knows how many were injured."

"Messiahs shouldn't be allowed to live in the city," Tchama declared.

"Don't let the wrong people hear you say that," Auntie Peg warned. "We're almost there."

After a little farther, they entered Shifton.

The sky was darkening and the air was brisk.

Tchama pulled her jacket tight as they approached the house.

Auntie Peg knocked on the door, and a moment later, Theolan opened it.

"Why, hello, lovely ladies! Please, come in!" He stepped back and bowed as they entered. "To what do we owe this unexpected delight?" he asked.

Auntie Peg leaned toward him and they gave each other air kisses. Then she said, "I hear you've got a new friend staying at the house, and I would love to meet them!"

The mystic and Ninyani came out from the back room.

Lahari's voice called from upstairs. "Who's here?"

Her father hollered back up to her, "It's Peggy!"

Auntie Peg turned toward the stairs and said in a bright voice. "Hey, gurl!"

"*Hey, gurl!*" Lahari repeated back down to her.

Auntie Peg reached out her hand to Ninyani, and he took it. "Hello, there," she said to him. "It is so delightful to meet you. I'm sorry, Tchama has told me your name already, but would you please remind me of it?"

The boy was starstruck. He stared up at Auntie Peg's large bouffant, her dramatic makeup, the billowing and cinched gown she was wearing. "Ninyani," he gasped in awe.

"*Ninyani,*" Auntie Peg dutifully repeated, "that is a beautiful name! You can call me Auntie Peg or Peggy." As she released his hand, she reached out and caressed the frilly pink and yellow scarf that was still wrapped around his neck. "And this is just lovely," Auntie Peg cooed.

The boy's face lit up.

"Tchama gave it to me," he declared.

"Well, I think it looks stunning on you!" Auntie Peg turned to the mystic and his husband. "I'm headed over to the Shady Lady, and I think our new little friend here would enjoy it. Do either of you have any interest in joining us?"

The mystic perked up and turned to his husband. "You don't mind if I tag along with them, do you, my dear?"

Theolan smiled from ear to ear. "I know how much you love a good show," he replied.

"Theolan, why don't you come, too?" Auntie Peg recommended.

"Oh, thank you," he replied with a grin, "but I'm very happy staying home with a good book. Maybe Lahari and I will play cards or do some cooking."

The mystic gave his husband a peck on the cheek and turned to Auntie Peg. "Peggy, let me change, and I'll be ready to go." He disappeared upstairs.

Auntie Peg looked back at Ninyani. "Would you like to tell me a little bit more about yourself?" she asked.

The two sat together, and Ninyani shared with her his life and answered some of her questions. A few minutes later, the mystic was in a fresh outfit that was brightly colored indeed.

"Ready!" he declared.

"I haven't even asked you yet," Auntie Peg said to Ninyani. "Would you like to join us and see a performance?"

He gave her an excited nod. "Will there be dancing?"

Auntie Peg stood, raised one hand above her head, and snapped her fingers. "There *better* be dancing!" she declared with a laugh.

Ninyani broke out with a beaming smile.

Auntie Peg led him, the mystic, and Tchama back out into the cold evening.

The busy streets were still bustling with people, and after a moment, they left the Shifton neighborhood.

Auntie Peg turned them down a side street toward a large crowd that was gathered not far ahead.

"Almost there," she informed the others with a smile. She looked down at Ninyani.

His eyes were wide and his mouth was agape with wonder.

"They're a fancy bunch, aren't they?" Auntie Peg asked him.

He looked up at her in amazement.

The crowd ahead was exuberant. People were cheering and chanting and cackling with glee, and a few of them were indeed dancing, right in the street. Music was coming from one of the nearby buildings.

Despite everything Ninyani was seeing, he could not take his eyes off the dancers. There were three of them in continuous movement, and their enthusiasm made others temporarily join in, and the dancers moved on to other partners. They danced in ways Ninyani had never seen before. They swerved and dipped and leapt through the air. They dropped and popped and bounced and bumped.

The formulaic and ritualistic dancing in Frostflower seemed rigid compared to the fluid and free movements of these dancers. Ninyani watched one of them approach a group of several men, and all of them suddenly joined in as well!

Ninyani burst out with a delighted laugh, and he covered his face with one dainty hand and blushed at himself. His eyes lingered on them as the dance continued, but the boy was suddenly taken aback by what else he realized he was seeing. The costumes, oh, the costumes!

Massive teased wigs donned people's heads. Glittering gowns flowed from bodies. Exaggerated makeup and gaudy jewelry decorated many of the gathered folk. Ninyani's eyes moved over the diverse variety of fashion. There were sequins and animal prints and ruffles; there was lace and leather and silk and satin.

"Gobsmacked, are we?" Auntie Peg asked with a knowing and playful smirk. She paused at the edge of the crowd, took a compact out of her purse, and opened it.

Ninyani watched her check herself in the mirror.

"A face dusted to perfection!" she proclaimed. "Should we give you a little something?" Without waiting for his reply, she offered, "How about a little gloss for your lips? Or maybe a touch of eye shadow or blush?"

Ninyani looked confused.

Auntie Peg smiled at him, then she grabbed the hand of someone in the crowd.

A mustachioed individual turned, beamed at Auntie Peg with recognition, and exclaimed, "Peggy!" The person wrapped her in a tight hug.

She laughed and replied, "I'd like you to meet our new friend, Ninyani." Auntie Peg released the embrace and turned toward the boy.

He looked up at the other person. She was wearing a dress and lots of makeup. However, a large handlebar mustache also graced her upper lip.

"Wow," Ninyani whispered, and Auntie Peg's friend gave the child a toothy smile.

"You can call me," she said in a deep voice, "Miss Cleopatra." She stroked her mustache.

"You're so pretty!" Ninyani replied.

Miss Cleopatra guffawed. "I should hope so!" she declared. "Look at all the time and effort that I put into *me*," and she struck a pose.

Ninyani giggled, and some people behind Miss Cleopatra applauded for her.

Tchama joined in with them and cheered.

"I was just offering Ninyani some makeup," Auntie Peg commented to Miss Cleopatra.

The mustachioed woman released her pose, and the cheering faded. Miss Cleopatra pulled an exaggerated look of surprise and proclaimed, "Of course, he wants some makeup! Let's beat that mug until it's sickening! Do you have any spare sparkles? The boy should be dripping in eleganza!"

Auntie Peg knelt beside the small boy and pointed up at Miss Cleopatra. "Would you like some lipstick, like her?"

Ninyani's eyes glittered with delight, and all he could do was nod *yes*.

"Thank you, Miss Cleopatra," Auntie Peg said.

Miss Cleopatra gave them an elegant curtsy and turned back to the crowd.

Auntie Peg reached into her purse and pulled out a case with three lipsticks in it. "How about just a touch of shimmer?" she offered. "You can go red, like Miss Cleopatra there, or if you'd prefer something subtler, I've got a soft pink. However, if you're in the mood for something crazy, I also have a stick of green lipstick!"

The boy looked like he could barely comprehend what he was being offered.

"Let's go for the soft pink," Auntie Peg suggested, "and see how you feel." She popped the cap and said, "Pucker your lips a little, like this." She demonstrated.

Ninyani followed her instruction, and she spread of thin layer of gloss across his bottom lip.

"Now, rub them together like this." She showed him again. Auntie Peg turned her compact toward Ninyani, and the boy saw himself in the mirror.

He stopped breathing.

"I agree," Auntie Peg said with a grin, as if reading his thoughts. "That looks just lovely! Why don't we go inside and see what all this commotion is about?" She shot him a mischievous grin. "You're in for a treat, my new friend. And I think you look marvelous just like that! Let's head in."

Ninyani and Tchama followed Auntie Peg into the club.

The mystic was laughing with a group of fancy-looking people, and he remained outside.

Ninyani tugged on Auntie Peg's sleeve and she looked down at him.

"Why did Miss Cleopatra say to beat me and make me sick?"

"Didn't you see yourself in the mirror?" Auntie Peg asked with a smirk. "You are sickeningly gorgeous! That's what she was saying," and she smiled at him.

The place was packed and Auntie Peg pushed through the dense crowd and made her way over to the bar. A few people greeted her by name and a couple of folks gave her air kisses on both cheeks.

An inebriated character was yammering loudly over people at the bar. Her bright pink wig was rather askew.

"Mrs. Venus," Auntie Peg said to her, "you're getting a little sloppy. Time for Madame Petunia to take you home."

Auntie Peg hoisted Mrs. Venus from her seat, and despite mumbling protests from Madame Petunia, Auntie Peg convinced her to take Mrs. Venus away. She then reached down to Ninyani, put her hands under his arms, and hoisted the boy off the floor. She planted his feet on the chair where Mrs. Venus was just sitting.

Ninyani stared at Mrs. Venus and Madame Petunia with a bemused expression, then he turned to Auntie Peg. He asked her, "Is Mrs. Venus a man?"

Auntie Peg burst out laughing. "Honey," she said to him in a pandering tone, and her voice dropped an octave as she replied, "most of us are." She gave the boy a beaming smile. Her voice returned to its normal timbre. "Mrs. Venus, Madame Petunia, Miss Cleopatra with her luxuriant mustache, and even yours truly are all *queens!* Underneath all of this fabulousness," and Auntie Peg waved her hands in front of herself, "there is indeed a boy hiding, but when I am all done up, I'm Peggy. I am exactly who I am supposed to be." She could see the wonder in Ninyani. "And don't you worry, you'll figure out who *you're* supposed to be also, my young friend."

Ninyani felt alive in a way he had never experienced before.

Movement caught his eye, and he carefully turned on his perch; Auntie Peg placed her palm against his back to help keep him steady.

The hall that they were in was large. At the opposite end from the bar was a stage with a catwalk that extended out into the middle of the crowd. What Ninyani saw there surprised and delighted him.

Two women were strutting across the stage. Both were in high heels. One was dressed in sheer lingerie that hugged her body, and a sparkling tiara was on her head. The other was only wearing a black thong and a very short jacket with a collar of thick white fur. The coat only came partway down the model's ribs, and her stomach, low back, and legs were bare.

The two women's sexy clothing and exposed bodies neither aroused Ninyani nor made him feel uncomfortable. Instead, he simply gazed in awe at their beauty. The spiked platform heels they both wore were tall, and the fancy footwear added to the women's impressive height. They towered over the cheering audience.

Music was playing, and it was almost drowned by the noises of the onlookers. Their praise for the pair of parading divas was overwhelming, and Ninyani could not help it, and he surprised himself when he cheered aloud. He brought both his little hands up and covered his mouth again in embarrassment.

Auntie Peg was looking at him with a wide smile, and she suddenly let out a whooping cheer for the women on stage. She leaned toward Ninyani and said, "The one with the skimpy jacket is my brother. Her name is Dame Angelica. She's not my biological brother, but when I first came here to Teshon City, she was the man who gave me a place to stay and helped me find the Auntie Peg who lived within me."

Ninyani asked again, "That's a man?"

"*Queen*," Auntie Peg corrected gently. "It sort of doesn't matter what's underneath," she explained, "but anyone can be a queen. When he's not Dame Angelica, he uses his regular name, but all dressed up, she's a queen! However, for the other woman up there with the see-through bodysuit, it's a little different. Her name's Zular, and she lives her entire life as a woman. Whether she's in costume and dressed up for a performance, or she's just going to the market for apples, she is always Zular."

"I don't understand," Ninyani said. "Does your brother not go to the store as Dame Angelica?"

"Very rarely," Auntie Peg replied, "usually he just goes as his *basic* self. However," and she pointed at the stage, "Zular is always Zular."

Ninyani scrunched up his face in concentration and asked, "Does that mean Zular used to be somebody else before she became Zular?"

Auntie Peg beamed at him. "That is an interesting question, but the answer is hers to tell. Maybe you'll get the opportunity to ask her someday. Zular is exactly who she is supposed to be. She's exactly who she *wants* to be, and anyone can do that. I am who I am supposed to be, even though I was born and raised to be very different than this," and Auntie Peg again brought her hands up the length of her body. She then framed her face and struck a dramatic pose for Ninyani.

He laughed at her display.

Then the music stopped, and the two women on the catwalk bowed and strutted backstage. Another song began. The curtain opened, and the master of ceremonies stepped out on the riser.

Ninyani's mind tried to describe the person in terms that he understood, and he thought to himself that he was looking at a man, but the fellow was in even higher heels than the two women who had just left the stage. He was also wearing fitted leggings that were striped in multiple shades of pink, with a matching pink bra, and no shirt. His chest and arms were very hairy.

A frizzy green wig was on the man's head, and despite several strong head-swishes, it did not move. His makeup looked less intentional than some of the other folks at the fundraiser, and more like he just slapped himself in the face with a handful of glitter. He absolutely sparkled. The man looked older than Auntie Peg or the mystic, but he pranced around the stage with youthful enthusiasm.

The onlookers hollered and whistled and cheered for him.

"What did you think of those two, then?" he asked the crowd, and they roared their approval and appreciation for the performers. "What a way to start the evening! Stunning!" he continued. "They're stunning! Our ladies are downright pummeling the catwalk tonight, and I am alive because of it! Give me life. Give it to me, now!"

The audience screamed.

"Up next," he declared, "our three models will be judged on their coiffeurs, on their..." he paused and took a dramatic breath, *"hair to the ceiling!"*

The crowd erupted and re-doubled its cheering, as the first woman walked onto the stage. She was in a corset and skirt that puffed out from her hips. Her legs were long, and her heels were high, but her hair was the main attraction. The blond wig that sat atop her head crowned her in an immense halo of gold. The hair stretched out to the sides wider than her shoulders, and it reached up above her head just as tall. It looked like a lion's mane, and when she turned her head, the wig moved with her.

Ninyani burst out laughing with delight from up on his chair, but then his jaw dropped as the second woman began strutting along the catwalk. Her hair was styled in rigid spikes that protruded in all directions from her head, and the spaces in between were completely bald.

"That is quite a wig," Auntie Peg commented to Ninyani. "Can't imagine how long it took to style."

The final performer stepped out onto the stage in multicolored locks that flowed all the way down to her ankles. She was skinny and tall, and her rainbow hair swept behind her like a cape.

"Stomp that stage!" Auntie Peg called out to the performers.

"Yeah!" Ninyani agreed, unsure of what he should yell.

Auntie Peg was delighted that the boy felt comfortable. She leaned over the bar and held up two fingers to the person behind it. A moment later, a pair of bright red beverages was placed before her.

"Here you go," she said to Ninyani. "Give that a sip. It's sun-cherry juice." She took a swig and smacked her lips at him.

*

While all the patrons at the Shady Lady were enjoying the fundraiser festivities, clear across Teshon city, a massive building ruptured and collapsed to the bedrock of the peninsula★

Chapter 18 – New Target

The dead of night was upon the land, and Teshon City was quiet.

"There it is," S'Kay said, and she pointed.

Eroli squinted through the darkness.

"That's it?" Gawa asked.

"You'll see," S'Kay replied.

The trio crept up to the side of a building, and they peered in through the cloudy glass of an old window. Crates lined the walls; several large objects that were covered in tarps stood in the middle of the space.

"How did you find this place?" Eroli asked.

"I first found it when I was a kid, living in the Spritehood, before I changed." S'Kay ruffled her feathers and continued. "I hadn't been to it in years and forgot about it entirely until we started this, but I came here last night and checked it out. Not only is it still a functioning warehouse for the Messiahs, but there are weekly shipments that come through. I found a manifold and a logbook."

The three Biological Shifts leaned in close together.

"There was a bunch of old Oselian equipment," S'Kay went on, "but nothing that seemed all that worthwhile, a crate of rusty helmets and other junk. There were sacks of coal and stacks of lumber. I don't really care what else is in there," she added, "I just want to ruin whatever operation they've got going. Destroying this building will disrupt whatever the Messiahs are doing."

S'Kay brought her hands to the wall in front of her.

"Each of you, go around to opposite sides," she instructed, "and let's tear it to the ground."✪

Chapter 19 – The Principal Messiah

"What do you mean *the Spritehood warehouse was destroyed?*" the Principal Messiah asked through gritted teeth. She glared at the officer who delivered the news.

It was barely sunrise.

"Affirmative, milady," the man said in a shaky voice. "We can't tell what happened, but the building collapsed."

"Was there anything of value in it?"

The man sucked air between his lips. "Well, it all had value, milady."

She snapped her reply at him. "Was anything important destroyed?!"

"I don't think so, milady. We haven't received any decent artifacts in months. There were some old formal military costumes, but nothing of real value. Where are we supposed to store this week's shipment when it arrives?"

"There's never more than a few crates at a time," the Principal Messiah growled, "so I expect you to figure it out. I want a full report before sundown," she demanded. "And find Vion. I want to see him, now."★

Chapter 20 Auntie Peg & Ninyani, Part One

After the fundraiser, it was late, and Auntie Peg brought Ninyani back to her home that was above her shop in the Spritehood. The mystic and Tchama both left earlier in the evening, but Ninyani wanted to stay until the very end of the event. Auntie Peg was happy to stick around with him, and she told the mystic that Ninyani could stay with her for the night.

The next morning, Auntie Peg asked Ninyani, "How would you feel about hanging out with me today? I suspect the boys will be helping with the injured in Gate Town. It's very kind that the mystic and Theolan have given you a place to stay."

"And Lahari," Ninyani added with a smile.

"Yes, indeed," Auntie Peg concurred, "but you are more than welcome to stay with boring old me as long as you'd like."

"You're not boring!"

Auntie Peg smirked. "Well done, you must remember to always give a compliment to someone who goes fishing for one," and she laughed. "Why don't we keep the shop locked up for the day and start out by making ourselves some breakfast?"

Ninyani perked up at the mention of food and asked, "Can I help you cook?"

"If that's something you'd like to do," Auntie Peg replied, "I'd love for you to assist me in the kitchen!"

They left the CLOSED sign on the front door of her shop, and the two spent the morning there, away from the destruction in Gate Town. Several times, Auntie Peg noticed people through the window, and she popped her head out the door to ask for details and updates about what was happening in the rest of the city. With the information she gathered, she decided that the two of them should remain at her house until things calmed down in Gate Town.

Morning became afternoon, and Ninyani and Auntie Peg enjoyed their day together. Soon it was evening, and Auntie Peg lit several lamps and set Ninyani up at her kitchen table.

"How would you like to make some jewelry?" she asked.

Ninyani's face lit up with delight.

"I thought you might enjoy that," Auntie Peg added. "Why don't you take a look at some of what I've made?" She placed a fancy case onto the table and lifted its lid. Two necklaces, three rings, and a pair of earrings were inside the box. Each was rustic with a handmade quality. "Go ahead," she urged.

Ninyani picked up each and examined them with sparkling eyes. "You made these?" he asked.

"I did, indeed!" Auntie Peg declared. "Do you want to try on one of the necklaces?" She helped him clasp a dainty chain behind his neck. "I bet *you're* able to make some lovely jewelry. I've got a whole case of interesting charms and pretty rocks and gemstones. We can use wire to make the settings or I have some clasps that will work."

Auntie Peg placed a large container that was made up of much smaller compartments in front of Ninyani, and she told him, "Peek inside each of those little boxes."

He found sparkling stones in a rainbow of colors. There were little charms of animals, suns and moons and stars, flowers, even skulls. He took his time and looked in every one of the compartments.

Auntie Peg sat across from him, working on a pendant that she had started earlier. Watching the boy made her smile; he could not decide where to start.

"So many of them are so pretty!" Ninyani declared. "I can't choose one!"

Auntie Peg chuckled and recommended, "So, then, pick a bunch of them. Make your jewelry as fabulous as you want it to be!"

Ninyani looked astonished. "I can use more than one?"

"That's up to you," Auntie Peg replied. "You might decide one stone or one little pendant is exactly what you want, but you might decide to go for a whole array of stones and dangly things." She leaned over the table toward Ninyani, put up her hand in a conspiratorial way, and whispered, "I don't know if you can tell, but I'm a little over the top!" She laughed and made a funny face at him and he giggled. She pointed at the necklace she made, now draped around Ninyani's neck. "That one's got five stones on it. Be as creative as you want to be," she told him.

Then there was a knock at the door✪

Chapter 21 – Dozi, Ilya, & Tchama

"Dozi, wake up," whispered a voice.

Dozi sat up with a start.

Tchama was kneeling beside her bed, right in front of Dozi's face.

"I'm sorry to wake you," Tchama said quickly, "but the neighborhood watch in Shifton needs volunteers right now! The Messiahs are back, and they are threatening violence. There's a huge crowd standing against them. The night's watch is leading the resistance, and they want whoever else they can get."

Dozi looked over at Ilya. She was already awake and rubbing her eyes, trying to pep herself up.

The two of them had spent a second day aiding the people in Gate Town, and they were both exhausted.

"I'm sorry," Tchama repeated. "I know that you haven't gotten much sleep."

"No, it's okay," Dozi mumbled.

"Yeah," Ilya agreed. She yawned and added, "we need to do what we can."

"I'm going to go check on Ninyani," Tchama told them, "and I'll meet you with the resistance afterward. He stayed with Peggy last night after the show, and he's been with her all day today. She's keeping him hidden while this chaos is going down in Gate Town."

Dozi nodded, and a moment later, Tchama was up the stairs and gone.

"I wonder how close it is to sunrise," Ilya said in a groggy tone. "I don't think we got nearly enough sleep."

"I think the sun only *set* a few hours ago," Dozi replied. "There's a lot of night left, but what we're doing in Gate Town is important. Let's go."

They headed out and made their way across the city.

"Why didn't we go with Tchama to see Peggy first, and then all three of us go to Shifton together?" Ilya asked.

"Because the watch needs people now. I get it that she's worried about Ninyani. She'll be along soon."

A few minutes later, Dozi and Ilya could again see fires burning and hear shouting voices. They crept down a side street and snuck into the neighborhood toward a crowd of people that included several Biological Shifts. Everyone was chanting for the Messiahs to keep out of Gate Town.

Across the street from them, a vicious group of Messiahs menaced in opposition, and the indistinguishable noise of too many screaming voices was a cacophony beneath the dark sky.

Dozi and Ilya took their place among the protesters.

"Fuck you, Messiahs!" Dozi jeered.

Ilya looked at her, impressed.

The Messiahs held their position against the much larger and unquestionably powerful group that resisted them. The protesters were causing the Messiahs to boil up into a rage, but still they did not attack.

The noisy stalemate lingered in the powder keg city, as minutes stretched toward an hour, and then two.

Dark was the night, and there were still many hours until dawn★

Chapter 22 – An Unexpected Guest

S'Kay, Gawa, and Eroli headed through the darkness onto the old Oselian airstrip near their secret hideout.

"We should be in Shifton!" Eroli declared. "They need our help!"

Gawa wore a look of concern on her face. The patterns that rippled across her skin moved in an unnerving way. "I'm worried about the resistance."

"They can take care of themselves," S'Kay replied in an icy voice.

"But we started all of this," Eroli mumbled miserably.

"Yes," S'Kay agreed, as she ducked under a warning sign, "we did start all of this," but then a loud voice that none of them were expecting spoke from inside their secret lair.

"And you cannot stop now."✪

Chapter 23 – Photonova Gland

"Making jewelry sounds like a lot of fun," Tchama said to Auntie Peg. The two of them were at the front door to Peggy's Potions. "But I told Dozi and Ilya that I would join them with the resistance. Oh, and Peggy, *you* should be there too, since you're a Messiah!"

Auntie Peg cringed and looked over at Ninyani with concern on her face. She was yet to tell him about her past, or that she was an ex-Messiah, and she worried about his reaction. However, the boy was unfamiliar with Messiahs, and the term meant nothing to him. He did not respond to Tchama's words at all.

Tchama again kicked herself and made a guilty expression at Auntie Peg for letting yet another secret slip, but Auntie Peg mouthed the words *It's okay*.

"I understand why you want me to be there," she said aloud to Tchama, and she nodded at Ninyani, "but staying out of sight is the course of action that he and I need to take. In fact, why don't you stay here with us?" she offered, but she continued without letting Tchama reply. "I can also understand why you think it's important to be in the resistance, but there are powerful individuals who are going to be facing off against the empowered. You're a human. I worry that it's going to be extremely dangerous for any humans."

"But I just sent Dozi over there! She and Ilya!"

"The two of them know what they're doing and what they are getting into. I won't force you to stay here," Auntie Peg said with a smile, "I just hope that you do."

"We're making jewelry!" Ninyani called to Tchama from the other room.

"See," Auntie Peg said, "I told you we're already having fun. Why don't you join us for just a little while? Make yourself a pair of earrings or a necklace, and then you can go on your way."

Auntie Peg let out a sigh of relief as Tchama entered. She closed the door behind her, locked it, then added in a tone that sounded a little deflated for the normally-upbeat woman, "There will always be more violence, Tchama."

Auntie Peg smiled and continued in her normal voice. "Head into the kitchen with Ninyani. There's wire for making the fastenings and some settings, and in front of him is a box with different types of stones and charms. I've only got two sets of tools for detailed work, so we'll need to share. Grab that chair and pull it over to the table. Have a seat beside Ninyani. Would you two like a cup of tea?"

"Yes, please," Ninyani replied.

"Thank you," Tchama said, "that would be nice."

A few minutes later they were sipping their warm beverages.

Tchama scoured the box of treasures and decided to make herself a new pair of earrings. She selected the posts she liked, picked out a pair of gemstones, and cut two pieces of wire. The minutes slowly slipped by as she formed one into a setting that would hold the first stone, but it was tedious work.

Tchama's mind kept drifting to Dozi and Ilya, as Ninyani discussed the previous night's fabulous fundraiser at length. Even though Tchama had been there with him, he still told her in great detail about the costumes and hair and makeup. He described the different performances and compared them to the folk dancing from his village. Ninyani spoke with fawning tones about the models who he thought were the most beautiful. He shared lyrics from songs that stuck in his memory, and even described the ways that he and Auntie Peg cheered for the show. The boy reminisced as if reliving his fondest memory.

Ninyani was already close with Tchama, and there was a special bond forming between Auntie Peg and the boy. He chatted to his little heart's content and got choked up for only a moment when the conversation turned to his mother, but Auntie Peg was quick to redirect the discussion.

At one point, Ninyani asked about Lahari, and Auntie Peg told him about her fascinating abilities, and where she used to live in the underground. Both Tchama and Ninyani were intrigued by Auntie Peg's details.

Tchama wanted to ask more about Lahari, because she knew very little about Lahari's life before they met. They became good friends over the half-year they had known each other, but Tchama knew that Lahari did not like talking about her life in the underground. Lahari was happy in Shifton with her fathers, and she did not care to relive her darker days, so Tchama knew very little about her time before they met.

Auntie Peg informed Ninyani and Tchama that she had been friends with the mystic and Theolan for over a decade, and the three of them were already close when Lahari hit puberty and her physical appearance began to change. Auntie Peg told them that Lahari was abused by her mother, and how her fathers helped her move into the underground.

"The details of the stories are hers to tell," Auntie Peg said. "Lahari has experienced some serious trauma, but she is an incredibly strong young woman. Let me get you both some more tea." she offered.

When she sat back down, the trio talked about Ninyani's childhood in Frostflower.

Auntie Peg told them about growing up in a cult and how she escaped as an adult.

Tchama talked about being brought to Teshon City as a child, but she was not interested in telling them much about that.

Eventually, an hour had ticked away, and Tchama was finally attaching the first earring post to the wire setting that she fashioned. She placed it onto the tabletop and stretched her arms overhead.

After a sigh, she asked Ninyani, "What do you think of the city so far? I know you've only seen a little of Teshon, but how do you feel living here?"

However, Auntie Peg interrupted, and she looked serious. She asked Ninyani in a quiet voice, "May I please see the lovely necklace you're making?"

The boy nodded and handed it to her with a proud smile, but Auntie Peg was clearly concerned.

"Where did you get this?" she asked in an unsettled voice.

Tchama turned to her. "What is it? That's not one of your crystals?" She pointed at the case full of stones.

Auntie Peg stared at the gem in her hand and replied with certainty in her voice.

"This is a mantis gland."

Tchama looked both startled and alarmed.

"What's that?" Ninyani asked.

"You don't know?" Auntie Peg responded.

The boy shook his head.

Auntie Peg looked over at Tchama and then back at Ninyani. "Well," she began, "as a matter of fact, you have one of these yourself, inside of you. Your photonova, or mantis gland, is what gives you your abilities over hot and cold. This crystal came from a Shift, someone like you or Ilya or Lahari. Where did you find it?"

Ninyani dropped his head in shame, as if a dark cloud had formed over him. He did not reply, and Auntie Peg took his little hand.

"It's okay, honey," she said in a gentle tone. "Whenever you're ready to tell us where this came from, we'll be ready to listen. However," she went on, "I don't think, despite how pretty it is, that this gemstone will make for the best necklace." She extended it back to Ninyani, but he was reluctant to take it.

"Let me explain," she continued. "This is what some people are after. This is the very special part of all Shifts, the thing that certain others would be willing to kill a person to get." She urged, "You need to keep it secret," and she placed it back in his hand.

Ninyani looked down at the crystal and asked, "I've got one of these inside of me?"

Auntie Peg nodded. "All Shifts have them. You've got one of those pretty little gemstones living right in the center of your head."

"I do?" he asked in a voice full of wonder.

"Yes, indeed you do," Auntie Peg replied. She reached out and touched the boy on his forehead. "Right in that little melon of yours, but if someone learns that you're a Shift, or finds out that you've got a loose mantis gland in your possession..." she trailed off before continuing.

Auntie Peg pointed at the sparkling stone in his palm. "Mantis glands are one of the most expensive gems in the world, and they are jealously sought after. There's a chance someone might try to take it from you." She placed her hand on his shoulder. "I don't mean to frighten or upset you, but there are people out there who would do bad things to have it," she reiterated. "So, as lovely as the necklace is, I really feel it would be best if you kept the gland hidden. You can use as many of the gems and stones from my collection as you'd like."

Ninyani's expression was serious. He removed the photonova gland from the setting he was making for it, tucked the gemstone back into his coin bag, and stuck it in his pocket.

"Why don't you see if any of these spark your fancy?" Auntie Peg offered, and she slid the box of decorative stones in front of him.

Ninyani got back to work.

Auntie Peg and Tchama made eye contact. They did not share with Ninyani the unspoken understanding that passed between them.

The three talked very little over the following hour, but eventually, Tchama finished the second earring and she laid the matching set onto the table in front of her.

"Finally! That took forever," she stated.

"It just requires a little practice," Auntie Peg replied, "and a little patience."

Ninyani yawned and rubbed his eyes. "I'm not done," he said, "but I'm getting sleepy." He placed his unfinished necklace beside Tchama's earrings and shuffled over to the couch Auntie Peg had set up for him as a spare bed the night before.

She got up from the table and helped him remove his bulky sweater, then she tucked him in and turned off the light. She returned to the kitchen with Tchama and closed the door.

"Where do you think he got that mantis gland?" Tchama asked.

"Maybe it was some sort of heirloom from his village," Auntie Peg guessed. "He said his people thought of Shifts as gods. Maybe it was some sort of precious artifact they were keeping."

"What could you do with that?" Tchama asked. "I know you're not a Demifae like the mystic, but you're in the healing arts, aren't there uses for a mantis gland that would help people? And isn't it dangerous for Ninyani to have it? Can't we put it away for him someplace safe?"

Auntie Peg took a deep breath and adjusted her corset. "I'm not going to take it from him. It's the last remnant of whatever life he used to have. I'll talk with him more about it tomorrow, and maybe he will want it to be used to help heal people, but I'm not going to force him or even encourage him to do anything with it. If he makes the decision on his own, I will tell him more about it then. Also," she added, "I don't think we should mention to anyone that he has it, not even Dozi or the mystic or anyone. The fewer people who know about it, the better."

She turned and selected a bottle of wine from a rack on the wall. "Would you like a glass?" she offered.

Tchama looked torn. "Dozi has been supporting the resistance in Gate Town for a couple hours already," she stated. "I really want to get over there and be a part of it, make some difference. The more people who show up, the more powerful the statement will be against the Messiahs."

"Please," Auntie Peg said in a gentle tone, "it will be violent. I really think you should stay here with us. I've got a big bed, you can sleep with me."

Tchama looked startled by the offer and blurted out, "I can't sleep with you!"

"Oh, honey, no!" Auntie Peg replied in surprise, and she burst out laughing, but she tried to subdue it so as not to wake Ninyani. "No, no, no, not like that. Honey, I don't have those kinds of feelings for women. I was just offering you a place to sleep." Auntie Peg smiled. "Tchama, you are totally safe with me."

"Erm, sorry, yeah, I know that," Tchama replied with a sheepish smile, but she felt reassured of her trust in Auntie Peg. "I don't know why I thought that. Sorry," she repeated. "Anyway, I just really want to go be a part of the movement."

"I won't stop you from going," Auntie Peg replied, "but I'm worried about any of you humans who get involved in a confrontation between such powerful beings."

"I'm not going to fight," Tchama reassured Auntie Peg. "I just want to be part of the crowd."

"Alright," Auntie Peg conceded, as she poured herself a glass of wine, "please, be careful!" she implored. She took a sip and sighed. "Bundle up, it's a cold night."

Tchama knew Auntie Peg was concerned, so she smiled reassuringly and said, "Don't worry, I'll be fine!"

Auntie Peg *was* worried. It felt like her warnings had not sunk into Tchama's heart. Alone again, she peeked into the dark room where Ninyani was peacefully sleeping, and her motherly eyes watched over his silhouette in the darkness★

Chapter 24 – The Clash

Vion wielded a sword.

Chenchi gripped a club.

They stood with 39 other Messiahs at the border to Gate Town. There was no sneak attack this time; they were bringing war to their sworn enemies.

The night was cold and dark, and the winter sunrise was still hours away. Countless voices, shouting at and over each other formed a raucous chorus that further built the tension.

Vion glared across at the resistance. There were many more people on the opposing side, and they looked to him like a ragtag mob of angry protesters, weak and ineffectual. However, there were undoubtedly Shifts, and he could even see several Biological Shifts. Vion focused on them.

He stared down to the far end of the resistance at a man with blue skin standing beside a figure who was transparent, not unlike the crystalline husks that Vion was investigating. He wondered if the two of them were part of the group who were killing his people.

As Vion left Chenchi and wove through the pack of Messiahs, he noticed a woman across the way whose hands burned with a pulsing red energy. He did not want to see what she could do; he wanted to cut off her head. Vion ground his teeth, hating the standoff, the stalemate that neither side seemed anxious to break. He continued through the crowd of Messiahs until he was across from the two Biological Shifts; Vion was determined to take their heads.

Then suddenly, a giantess lumbered up behind the inhabitants of Gate Town.

Vion stopped in his tracks. He was amazed.

The massive woman towered over everyone. She was wearing thick plate armor and carrying a wicked warhammer.

Vion wanted to cut her down to size, and he squeezed his sword's hilt in his powerful fingers. He also noticed a man in the crowd with smoke rising from his skin. The idea of slaughtering every enemy was delicious to Vion.

The far end of the two crowds erupted in chaos.

A beam of blue energy blasted into the Messiahs, and the screams of those who were hit by the assault rang out through the streets.

Vion could see what looked like a man-bear. The beast was not as big as the giantess, but he was huge.

Across from him, two Messiahs were on the ground, writhing in agony. They were both missing flesh and their exposed bones were scorched and blackened. One of them had been hit in the arm and the other in the ribs.

Seeing their catastrophic injuries, Vion assumed the man-bear was one of the killers he was hunting. He was now certain that the three murders were there in the Gate Town crowd, and the fiercest rage boiled up in him.

"*Charge!*" Vion screamed at his horde of Messiahs, and they did.

Several in the back of their group carried ranged weapons, and they hurled javelins like missiles into the protesters. Multiple people were impaled, both Shift and their human cousins alike. A pair of Messiahs at the back started throwing boulders into the resistance, and the rest of their fellow empowered brethren launched themselves at the residents of Gate Town.

Those humans among the protesters who possessed the greatest survival instinct fled the slaughter, but Shifts of all sorts retaliated against the Messiahs. Their energies appeared in countless forms.

Rings of yellow light flashed from one woman's hands. Another fired beams of green energy from her heart. The bear-man launched several more blue blasts, and from behind him, a young teenager with skin like liquid mercury jumped at an oncoming Messiah. The youth's body split into countless pointed projectiles that separated and soared through the air. They sank into the Messiah's nigh-invulnerable flesh and pierced him straight through. He fell dead, as the boy's liquid body reintegrated. His hands formed into a pair of long blades, and he rushed at the attackers.

Vion saw Chenchi collide with the resistance before he lost sight of her. Then he turned his gaze forward and ran at the Biological Shifts who dared to oppose his authority. He hoped they were the murderers, and he looked forward to massacring them.

The Biological Shift with blue skin reached out for Vion as he attacked, and the Messiah swung his sword through the air like a hurricane. The blade made contact, sinking into the blue man from his collarbone to his ribs. Vion's blow took the man's arm off, and it opened his torso with a monstrous fissure in his flesh. Pale yellow blood burst from the destructive strike, and vile organs the color of unripe tomatoes poured from the body-rending gash. He fell to the pavement.

Vion turned and swept his sword toward the transparent Biological Shift, and it collided with the man's neck. To Vion's astonishment, a full third of the blade snapped off with a ringing *krang* as it collided against the man's diamond-hard epidermis.

A crystalline fist like a jackhammer then slammed into Vion's mouth. The Biological Shift's other hand came crashing into his gut. Vion staggered back, shocked that a mere physical attack hurt him. He brought a hand to his face and was startled to see blood on his fingertips. This was the first time he shed blood since consuming the mantis gland that turned him into a Messiah.

He was further astounded, as the blue Biological Shift's body fused, and the man pushed himself up with his remaining arm. He then reattached the severed one, and the man's healing was instantaneous; he was back in the battle.

People in every direction were screaming. Unlucky humans who were caught in the path of the raging Messiahs were pummeled and left to die. Shifts who were unable to resist the assault fell to the strength of their enemies. Many Messiahs on the opposite side were struck by the eldritch cosmic energies of different Shifts, and they were destroyed.

Vion charged at the blue man again with his broken sword, but the giantess leapt in the way and swung her hammer down with the force of an avalanche. Vion caught himself and stumbled back as her weapon hit the pavement. The blow cleaved a massive divot in the thick concrete and caused a shockwave that knocked Vion to his knees and sent a stony shrapnel spray that pelted his skin.

He rose and roared, but the giantess was on to other enemies, and Vion found himself face to face with an unimpressive-looking elderly woman in an apron and a bonnet. She stepped right in front of him with a disapproving expression on her wrinkled face. Vion swept his sword through the air, and he laughed aloud, as the little old lady raised her hands to block the blade. His voice died, however, when her fingers did indeed stop the sword.

The woman gripped into the already broken blade, and to Vion's surprise, she twisted the metal as if his weapon were made of no more than folded paper.

"You're..." he stammered. "You're a..." but Vion was not given the opportunity to call her a traitor.

Distracted by the little ex-Messiah woman, another diamond punch slammed against the side of Vion's head and sent him sprawling. The crystal Biological Shift then kicked him in the guts and knocked the wind out of him. He collapsed to the pavement, gasping for breath, and hands grabbed Vion from behind. His eyes would not focus for a moment, and he thought that this would be his end, but he was yanked along the pavement, away from another felling blow of the giantess' hammer.

Above Vion's head, a void opened in the atmosphere like a disc of shadow, and a vicious bolt of black fire blazed from it. It grazed Vion's shoulder and he winced in agony. The pain was so severe that even with the breath still knocked from his lungs, he still managed to wheeze a pathetic cry. However, the hands that pulled him away now barely gripped him. Vion turned to look behind him. His eyes focused. The arms were still there, as were the legs, but the rest of his fellow Messiah's torso and head were vaporized to nothing.

Vion pushed himself to his knees again and shuffled to the edge of the battle. He slipped down a side alleyway, choking and gasping and slowly catching his breath. He pushed himself up, leaned against the wall, and stared back into the pandemonium.

The giantess' warhammer collided with a Messiah's head, and Vion watched his companion decapitated before his very eyes. He could not believe the woman's massive strength overpowered even that of the Messiahs.

Radiant bursts of energy filled the streets of Gate Town with multicolored explosions.

Vion could see Chenchi through the chaos, as many beams of power from multiple Shifts struck her down. The frail-bodied people in the resistance were slaughtered by the Messiahs, but the screams of Vion's brethren made him flee the battle. Their bodies were torn asunder by energies from the universe that they could not understand and not withstand.

Vion thought things were already bad, but they were about to get worse.

As he hobbled away from the violence, the Messiah Tower came into view. His relief turned to terror, as the temple of his people began to crumble and fall to the earth✪

Chapter 25 – Dozi

Dozi ran through the Shifton streets away from the violence in Gate Town. She abandoned the battle as soon as the fighting began. Her pulse raced, and her breathing was shallow. Tears streamed down her cheeks from the shock of it all. She did not want to die.

"Fucking Messiahs," she growled between her panting breaths.

At the start of the chaos, a giant chunk of masonry soared through the air and smashed into a man who was standing beside Dozi, crushing him like an insect. Speckles of his blood now decorated her shoes with its gory hue.

In the distance, she could still hear the confrontation. The screams and cries of the injured and dying rang out, punctuated by the strange sounds that accompanied each unique energy fired from the different Shifts who were involved in the battle.

Dozi did not know where she was running. The mystic's house was closest and she headed there, even though more than anything, she wanted to be safe in her secret basement home.

A crowd of people who were also fleeing the battle came barreling out from another street.

Dozi ducked down an alley to avoid drawing attention to herself, and she looked back to see if they were running from an immediate threat.

A horrible, axe-wielding brute of a man came charging behind them, and two armed Messiah women were with him. He swung his weapon down on a man, cutting him from neck to navel, and his mutilated body opened like some sort of twisted flower. The dead man's head lolled to one side and the corpse slumped to the pavement. The Messiah then swept his axe up like a volcano erupting. His huge curved blade gouged into a woman's torso, and her entire body lifted into the air. Her chest ruptured, and her ribs burst forth from the gash. She was dead before her body hit the ground.

Dozi was horrified, but she could not peel her eyes away from the violence.

Suddenly, a gigantic woman stepped out from a side street behind the Messiahs, and she grabbed the man by his head. He tried to swing his weapon at her, but she snatched it from him. The axe looked like a toy in her huge hand. She roared, thrust his weapon into his chest, and she twisted it. Then the giantess pulled on his head and ripped it from his body. His spine remained attached to his skull, and the massive woman used it like a whip. She slashed with his empowered spine at the other Messiahs.

Expecting to be unharmed by mere chunks of bone, the two women charged the enormous Biological Shift, but her makeshift weapon ripped into their flesh. The spine tore huge chunks from their torsos, and they screamed in agony that they could not have possibly imagined.

In the alleyway, Dozi was overwhelmed by everything she witnessed, and she vomited hard onto the pavement. Her head was spinning, but as the violence moved away from her hiding place, she pushed herself onward and finally came to the mystic's house. The door was locked, so she snuck around the back and sat alone while she tried to compose herself. Her eyes were streaming with tears.

Dozi did not know how long she sat alone, but she was far enough away from the battle that she could no longer hear it. With sunrise slowly illuminating the world, there was a knock on the front door. Dozi got up and crept back around the house.

"*Ilya!*" she cried out when she saw who it was. Dozi ran up to her, and they wrapped their arms around each other. "Are you okay?!"

"The fighting is over," Ilya replied. She whispered. "It was terrible. Are you by yourself? Have you seen Tchama or Lahari or anyone?"

"No, I'm the only one here," Dozi replied. "I've been hiding out in the back this whole time. Once people started dying, I just ran."

"You made the right decision," Ilya responded. "There are apparently still some lone Messiahs roaming the streets, so a bunch of Shifts and people are out looking for them."

The nearby shrieking of a woman pierced the quiet of the early morning.

"Help me! *Help!*" and the voice screamed in pain.

"Is that?" Dozi asked, and she and Ilya raced in the direction of the cries.

"Please, no. Please, no," Ilya started repeating to herself.

A chilly drizzle began to fall on the city, as the two women rounded the corner, and their worst fears in that moment turned out to be true★

Chapter 26 – The Tower

"Who's in there?" Eroli barked from behind Gawa, as S'Kay cautiously entered their hidden hideout.

"Oh," S'Kay exclaimed in surprise, "it's you!"

Gawa was clambering through the entrance behind her and declared, "I can't tell who it is." She then saw the unexpected guest. "What are you doing here?" Gawa asked.

S'Kay added, "How did you even find this place?"

"*Who is it?!*" Eroli snapped at the others as he entered.

He came to a halt, face to face with Lahari.

"Tualu came to me," she said, "and he brought me here. I could tell that someone else had been here recently, and when he left me alone, I figured I should just wait." Lahari looked from one of them to the next. "I've only been alone here for maybe five minutes. He must have known you were headed this way."

"But why did Tualu bring you to our hidden space?" Eroli asked.

"Isn't it obvious?" Gawa replied. "He thinks we need Lahari. We are going to do something important."

"I'm also curious," S'Kay added. "Why *did* he bring you here?"

"Well," Lahari replied, "since Tualu doesn't speak, and I don't know what you lot are up to, I'd say that *my* curiosities are more pressing. Now, what have you three been doing of late?"

Lahari stayed quiet as her fellow Biological Shifts recounted the details of their recent actions against the Messiahs of Teshon City.

When they finished, there was a quiet moment before Lahari stated, "250 years," and she took a breath. "For 250 years, our people have been hunted down and slaughtered." She paused and added, "I know why Tualu brought me here."

"You do?" asked Gawa.

S'Kay and Eroli looked at Lahari expectantly.

"Yes." Lahari smiled. "It's been a year since the Messiahs destroyed our home. A handful of them turned their backs on their fellow Messiahs initially, but the ones who've remained have doubled down on their cruelty. We are going after the Principal Messiah," she informed the trio. "We will kill everyone we find until their leader has been slaughtered, and we're not waiting. With the battle in Gate Town between the Messiahs and our kin, now is the time."

Eroli began to protest, but the three women stared at him with determination, and he conceded.

Moments later, the four of them were outside on the old Oselian airstrip. By making their way along it and staying outside of the city, they were able to position themselves only a few blocks from their destination.

A cold winter rain began to fall.

The quartet slipped up over the wall that led back into the streets, and they made their way along a dark alleyway to the base of the Tower. Without warning, Lahari stepped out and caught a pair of Messiah guards off-guard. Despite their empowered bodies, they were no match for her. The Biological Shift woman with energies like a black hole consumed their lifeforce with brutal devastation. The two were incapable of screaming in the agony they felt, as their very beings began to implode. Their dry flesh withered and clung to their bones. Lahari left them sprawled on the street, like a pair of mummified corpses, but both of them were still breathing.

She stepped up to the Messiah Tower and slipped inside. The other three vigilantes followed her between the massive Oselian steel slabs of the doors.

There was no one within.

Lahari pointed at S'Kay and Eroli, and then at the stairs that led to a basement level. They began to descend, as she and Gawa headed up in the opposite direction.

Another guard was at the top of the flight, standing in front of a large door. Again, Lahari walked right up to the startled man. She took hold of his face and one of his wrists, and he let out the smallest sound, barely more than a breath, as she pulled every particle of power from him. His eyes sank into his skull and his lips peeled back from his teeth; his fingers became skeletal, and he who was once formidable fell to the floor like a living skeleton. His ribs rose and fell weakly with his lingering existence.

The door he was guarding would not open for Lahari, but when Gawa unleashed her violet electricity into it, the metal crumbled and fell to a pile of corroded pieces. They entered and a strange smell hit them. Lahari flicked on the lights.

They were both shocked to see the unconscious man with tubes that connected him to several gruesome machines. The sight of him was disturbing, but also heartbreaking. They recognized him.

"That's the old barkeep from Red Raven's," Gawa whispered. "He's been missing for months. What are they doing to him?"

Lahari walked up to two of the machines and put her hands on them. With the shrill sound of tearing metal, they crumpled in on themselves, and the equipment was utterly destroyed.

No longer kept chemically incapacitated, the man gasped and his eyes flashed open. He flailed and almost fell off the table.

Gawa grabbed him on one side and Lahari held him on the other.

"It's us, Gawa and Lahari," she whispered. "Remember, we used to see you at Red Raven's? We're going to get you out of here."

Realization hit the man in an instant.

"No!" he snapped back, but his voice was full of urgency. "You have to destroy it. I'm not the only one. This isn't the only room." His eyes rolled and his head swam from the tortures he had suffered.

"Stay with us," Lahari said, and she slapped his cheek.

He focused again, and repeated, "You have to destroy it. Leave me," he pleaded. "The only way you can save me and the rest of us who are trapped in here is to destroy it. I'm already dead, we all are, the machines are the only thing keeping us alive. They don't just want our mantis glands; they are eating different parts of us, testing their reactions. Please," he begged, "destroy the Tower." Then he whispered to them in a voice full of sorrow, but also relief, "Go." His life was slipping away right before their eyes, and he yelled, *Go!*"

Lahari and Gawa turned their backs on him and descended toward the basement. They found S'Kay and Eroli on their way back up.

They looked terrified.

"There are three people down there," Eroli said through his teeth. "They are attached to machines!"

"We can't tell if they're Shifts or humans," S'Kay added, "but the Messiahs are doing something to them!"

Lahari put up her hand and replied, "We know."

Gawa nodded and informed S'Kay and Eroli, "We found the man from Red Raven's who disappeared a while ago. We woke him up and he told us the Messiahs are experimenting on Shifts, and there's no saving them; the machines are all that's keeping them alive." She added, "They're… they're already dead."

Lahari said to the others, "You know what we have to do."

"Outside," S'Kay commanded, and they followed her.

"Take up the cardinal positions," Lahari directed. "Eroli, go to the east. Gawa, the west. S'Kay, south," and Lahari took the north. "Give it everything!" she shouted, and the four of them unleashed their energies into the stone of the Messiahs' temple.

It stood for over two centuries, first above the Oselian base, and then above Teshon City. In its heyday, the Tower was a proud structure, but after the fall of Oselia, the concrete sentinel became one of the most feared buildings in the city.

Above Lahari's head, the wall of the Tower suddenly appeared to have been pelted with something, but nothing collided with the stone. Little divots of the old concrete burst, and they rained down as grey dust onto the street around her.

The walls above Eroli began to spiderweb multiple cracks like an early spring icy pond.

S'Kay poured her energies up the walls, and the very matter of the Tower started to compromise and dissolve.

Gawa sent her purple electricity radiating towards the structure's summit, and under the attack of the four, the building ruptured.

"*Run!*" Lahari screamed, and the four of them did, each in a different direction.

The Messiah Tower seemed to move in slow motion, buckling then bursting and slowly dropping like a waterfall of stones to the city streets. A raging torrent of dust swirled out in all directions like a tidal wave, and the four Biological Shifts raced away from the devastation✪

Chapter 27 – Tchama

Tiny droplets of cold rain began to drip from the sky, and Tchama pulled up her hood. The city streets were dark and quiet as she made her way from Auntie Peg's home in the Spritehood, but a low noise began to rise. It sounded like a strange hum, and Tchama was almost certain she could feel the vibrations in her feet. She stopped walking and realized the sound was indeed coming from the concrete below her.

Tchama continued on her way and turned onto a long path that led beside the old airfield. Down the first side street, she was startled to notice a thick cloud that looked like fog. Something about it was alarming, and it was moving toward her at a rapid pace. Tchama suspected it was not simply water vapor, and she hurried away.

Every time she looked back over her shoulder, it was a little closer. She decided to run. When she reached the edge of Gate Town, Tchama started zigzagging through the neighborhood away from the unnerving cloud.

Then she began to hear the cries of the dying, and she arrived at the site of the battle. Chaos reigned, and corpses were strewn about the street like rag dolls. Tchama froze when she saw the fighting. She slipped into an alleyway and hid behind a stack of crates. Tears flooded her eyes as she witnessed the numerous mutilated bodies. She saw people cleaved by Messiahs who wielded horrible weapons, and Shifts who eviscerated Messiahs with their cosmic energies.

Tchama watched the slaughter from her hiding place for more than two grueling hours, until very few from both sides were left standing. When she dared to move, she knew exactly where to go. The mystic's house was not far. She crept down the streets of Gate Town toward the entrance of Shifton. The winter sun was beginning to rise, and the drizzle gave everything a shimmer in the light of the dawn.

As Tchama turned a corner, she came face to face with a Messiah woman covered in blood. She was carrying a pair of short swords, and she charged at Tchama, who screamed and sprinted away. The woman was right on her heels, but only one thing filled Tchama's mind, getting to the mystic's house. She did not know how that would save her from an empowered enemy, but her fear stole from her the capacity to think of anything except getting to a place that had always been safe before.

Her feet pounded the pavement through Shifton toward the street where the mystic lived with his daughter and husband. Tchama rounded the last corner with the bloody Messiah woman close behind her, reaching for her.

"Help me! *Help!*" she screamed, but then blinding pain enveloped her, and Tchama slipped toward unconsciousness★

Chapter 28 – Tchama, Part Zero

On the night of the solstice that previous summer, Tchama had stayed up drinking as the late evening sun slowly set. She drank too much, then went wandering through the Teshon City streets. Her wobbly steps caused her to stumble down an alleyway, and her jacket got snagged on an old fan cage. She tugged at it drunkenly, but then she paused and noticed a low entrance that led somewhere unseen.

The pavement sank down underneath a portion of wall that stuck out and kept the opening almost entirely hidden. Tchama yanked her jacket and it ripped away from the cage. She ignored her torn garment and dropped to her knees. Her inebriated clumsiness caused her to slip below the wall onto the lower level of pavement, and she found herself right in front of what turned out to be a large secret door.

Tchama's eyes would barely focus, and she pushed herself up against it.

The door opened.

She stuck her head inside and slurred words into the dark basement. *"S'aneeeebody therrrre?!"*

Tchama got no reply and shuffled down the stairs. Her feet slipped out from under her on the last step and she fell hard on her backside.

"Ooof! Schtuuupid schtairs," she mumbled. Tchama stood and rubbed her sore prat. "S'there any booooze down'ere?" she asked to no one.

Suddenly, she heard voices from above, and she ducked down against the side of a bed.

Two young women descended. They were laughing and in mid-conversation. One of them lit several candles, and the other stopped talking right in the middle of her thought.

"Erm… there's a girl hiding behind the bed," she said. She was tall and muscular.

The other one turned like a flash and locked her eyes on Tchama. "Who are you?" she snapped. She was dressed in far too much clothing for summer. "How did you find this place? Where'd you come from?"

"I'mmm not tellin' you nuffin'bout anyfing!" Tchama declared almost incoherently.

"I think she's drunk," the taller one said.

"Don't get sick on our stuff," the shorter one added.

"I'mmm not drunk! Youuuu are!" Tchama retorted. "I'm not gonna be sick!" Then a surprised look came to her face. "Oh," she squeaked, "but I'mmm'parently pissin' my pants."

"What?!" squawked the overdressed one.

"Schorry," Tchama said with a shrug. She let out a contented sigh of relief.

"Gross."

"I'll get a towel," the tall one said. "Here, give me those clothes." She reached for Tchama.

For some reason, Tchama lashed out at her. Balling her fist, she punched the woman in her shoulder. Tchama's hand might have hurt from the impact, but her booze-bleary mind could not focus.

"What the fuck?" barked the short one.

Tchama repeated herself. "Schorry," she slurred. "Dunno why I did that." She gave her knuckles a suspicious glance. "Never done that before."

The tall woman looked at the shorter one with a smirk. "I'm fine," she said.

Then she turned back to Tchama. "I'm Ilya. That's Dozi. This is our house."

"Well, I'mmm not telling youuu nuffin' at all!"

Dozi rolled her eyes.

"Calm down," Ilya said to Tchama. "We're not gonna hurt you. You need to lay down, but let's get you clean before we put you to bed."

"She's not sleeping in my bed," Dozi declared.

"She can sleep in mine," Ilya replied, "and I'll sleep next to you."

"Great," Dozi mumbled in a tone thick with sarcasm.

"Oh, cheer up," Ilya urged. "She's just a kid and she's wasted."

"I'mmm notta kid! I'mmm turning eighteee..." but her voice trailed off.

"80?" Dozi asked with an incredulous expression.

"No, no, no," mumbled Tchama, "nex' week I turrrn 18!"

Dozi tutted. "Well, you're a mess, and you look like a child."

"*Yer a mess!*" Tchama snapped.

Ilya snorted a laugh. "Get her some clothes," she said to Dozi. "Look," she continued, turning back to Tchama, "since you won't tell us your name, can I just call you *Flower* for the time being? When I was a little girl, and first came to the city, I didn't tell anyone my name either, and a kindly old lady took me in who called me Flower. Can I just call you that, so I don't have to say *hey you* to you?"

Tchama was struggling with how to respond to the kindness that Ilya was showing her. She was not used to kindness. Life in Teshon City was hard.

Tchama was born to the south in the fishing village of Brokenpointe. Her mother did not speak about her father; the man was long gone before Tchama could remember him. She grew up playing with the other children of the town, but in her 11th year, the blood corruption developed in her mother. She was dead soon after.

An aunt who Tchama had never met took her in, and she moved with the woman to the big city. She lived close to the water, south of the Messiah Tower, and it became young Tchama's daily task to catch their food from the Grey Shallows.

The countless dead who fell in those tidal flats during the forgotten confrontations of the great Oselian Empire had provided food for a host of marine life. Those old corpses were long-devoured, but colonies of crustaceans and schools of fishes still lived in those shallows, and they provided an abundance to the residents of Teshon City.

Tchama would catch harbor crabs and quite a few different fish species that were decent for eating. She often came across sea urchins and oysters in the tidal pools, and she constructed a makeshift trap that could catch and hold a few shrimp at a time. She became quite a skilled little fisherwoman because it kept her outside, and she hated her time in her new home.

The city itself did not bother her, but her aunt was not a pleasant woman to be around. She drank heavily, and would occasionally slap young Tchama over trivial offenses.

Tchama learned to stay away, and she made acquaintance with a number of other folks who also fished for their meals. There was a big man that everyone called Papa J, who loved to tell stories. Tchama enjoyed setting up near him. She liked listening to him ramble about his past and his recitations of whatever fairytales he remembered from his childhood. Papa J's beard was long, and he wore a bow in it at all times. There were other regular fisherfolk who Tchama grew accustomed to, and she spent longer hours with them than she did with her aunt.

Life with the woman lasted a tedious six years, until one day near the start of summer, when Tchama returned home with their dinner. It was immediately clear to her that the blood corruption, which had killed her mother, was festering in her aunt, and it was already starting to debilitate the woman. There was only a matter of time before she would be gone. Tchama watched her deteriorate over the following several days, and when she knew death was close, she asked Papa J what to do with her aunt's body.

"Dump her in them there Grey Shallows," the man instructed. "That patch of ocean is made for the dead."

When the time came, Papa J assisted Tchama in moving her aunt's corpse to the cove. She spoke no words over the body as it began to sink, and after thanking Papa J, she returned to the empty house.

Despite the unpleasant life she lived with the woman, on the first night alone without her aunt, Tchama sobbed herself to sleep. The next day, she realized there were several bottles of alcohol that her aunt did not finish before becoming ill, and Tchama tapped into them herself.

Over the next several days, she took to drinking herself into a stupor, and on the eighth night of her inebriation, she decided to go stumbling through the city streets. That was when her jacket got hooked on the old fan cage, and she stumbled upon Dozi and Ilya's basement home.

In the flickering candlelight, Tchama stopped struggling and allowed Ilya to help her out of her damp trousers. She wiped herself down with the towel they gave her, and Ilya helped her dress in the clothes that Dozi provided.

Then Ilya put Tchama in her own bed, and she was unconscious as soon as she was on her back.

"She's a fucking disaster," Dozi declared.

"Yes, she is," Ilya agreed in concern. "Seems like she could use some friends."

The next morning, Dozi and Ilya were awake much earlier than Tchama. When she eventually did rise, she was hungover.

"Where am I," she groaned.

"Hi," Ilya said, "good morning, remember us? I'm Ilya and this is Dozi. Do you want some food? Are you hungry?"

"Ugh, no," Tchama replied, "food sounds terrible." She squeezed her eyes shut and rubbed her temples. "Do you have any alcohol?"

Dozi scoffed.

Ilya frowned and said, "That's one thing you don't need any more of, but how about coffee? Or even just water?"

"But the alcohol will kill my hangover," Tchama whined.

Dozi ignored her. "Will you at least be telling us your name, this morning?" she asked.

"Nope," Tchama huffed.

Dozi tutted and rolled her eyes.

"Where are you living?" Ilya asked.

Tchama looked around the basement. "Where am I?"

"This is my home," Dozi replied. She stepped up beside Ilya. "We live here together, and you are not supposed to know where it is."

"I *don't* know where it is," Tchama retorted in a bratty tone. "You haven't told me where we are."

"Sassy," Ilya said, "I like her."

Dozi rolled her eyes again.

Ilya sat on her bed near Tchama's feet. "Why don't you tell us where you live? That way we can be friends. You don't need to spend your nights drunk."

Tchama felt judged. "I can get drunk if I wanna get fucking drunk," she snapped. "Who are you to tell me what to do? I don't know you, and I don't owe you a thing."

"You could at least thank Ilya for letting you sleep in her bed last night," Dozi said with a scowl.

"Just let me get the fuck out of here."

Ilya chuckled to herself. "She swears as much as you do, Dozi."

"Do you want your pissy clothes?" Dozi asked in a snotty tone, as Tchama clambered out of the bed and started to shuffle toward the bottom step.

"Keep them!"

"Sweet kid," Dozi commented to Ilya, as Tchama climbed the stairs and slipped out the hidden door. "How do we know she's not gonna come back?"

"That has to have been embarrassing for her," Ilya replied. "I suspect we won't be seeing her again, and the basement is hard to find. She was drunk out of her mind when she stumbled on it."

"I don't fucking trust her," Dozi stated.

Ilya laughed. "You don't trust anyone to begin with!"

The day passed uneventfully, but late that night, Tchama snuck back to Dozi and Ilya's home. She counted on them again being out, and when she saw that there was no light in the cellar, she entered.

Dozi awoke to shuffling noises and sat up in the darkness, and she saw Ilya's silhouette upright in her bed. Dozi pointed toward the sound and nodded. She jumped up and lit a candle, as Ilya activated her powers of flight, and she slammed Tchama into the wall.

Dozi stepped over with the faint light from one of her candles.

"Oh, it's you, again," Ilya said above Tchama's dazed form. "Well, sorry about that. I guess I've more than made up for the punch last night."

Dozi snatched Tchama's bag. "What the fuck is wrong with you?" she snapped. "Why are you stealing my things?" and she pulled her belongings from the bag.

"Easy," Ilya interjected, and she looked at Tchama, "you came back because you felt safe with us, didn't you, Flower? What were your plans for…" and she looked over at the items in Dozi's hands, "two chipped teacups, a watch that needs a replacement battery, and a figurine of death?" Ilya looked up at Dozi. "What is that little stature anyway? I've been meaning to ask you about it."

"It's just a representation that people in my village make of the grim reaper. There were probably similar ones at the market in town." She scowled at Tchama and asked. "What were your plans with all my stuff?"

Ilya ignored Dozi and knelt down by Tchama. "What do you need, Flower?" she asked. "Do you need help? A place to stay? Food?"

"Whoa, whoa, what's all this about a place to stay?" Dozi retorted.

Ilya gave her a reproachful look and turned back to Tchama. "Are you alone?" she asked.

Tchama's hard facade cracked, and she burst into tears.

Dozi also softened, and she mumbled to herself, "Ugh, fine." She squatted down beside Ilya and put her hand on Tchama's shoulder.

"You gotta lay off the booze," Ilya recommended.

"Do you want something to eat?" Dozi offered, but Tchama just sobbed.

"It'll be okay, Flower," Ilya comforted.

Tchama was not used to such kindness.

When she was calm, they fed her and learned her name. Tchama told Dozi and Ilya about her sorrows and shared with them her broken life. That was the first night she stayed with them. The following morning, Dozi and Ilya went with Tchama to her empty house and collected the few things that were essential to her.

Tchama soon came to learn that she gained much more than just two friends; she was now part of a family, a real family. She was introduced to the mystic and his husband, Theolan, and Tchama was given ample warning and time to prepare before meeting Lahari. When she did, Tchama was fascinated with the unique Biological Shift woman. They quickly became fast friends, developing a connection that surprised Lahari in particular.

Tchama was happy for the first time in a long time.

Six months later, Messiahs attacked Gate Town.

Tchama was lying in the street. She was missing an arm.

Ilya was holding her broken body, and Dozi was kneeling beside the two women. She was recounting the story of their meeting and trying to help keep Tchama conscious.

Her wounds were severe and death was fast-approaching✪

Chapter 29 – Alone

Lahari found herself at the edge of the airfield.

Eroli skirted along the coast at the tip of the peninsula and headed north toward the old airstrip.

S'Kay slipped through the streets to Teshon City's southern edge. She followed it west all the way past the industrial district and turned north toward Gate Town.

Gawa ended up near the old Oselian barracks and did not recognize the area. She ducked down an alley, grabbed a tarp from a pile of garbage, and wrapped herself in it to hide her unique appearance. Voices came from the main street, and Gawa waited. A group of people headed by in mid-discussion. She could not tell what they were talking about, and they were soon gone. Gawa did not like being so unfamiliar with this region, and she moved with haste along a dark street. She rounded a corner and crashed into a group of two men and a woman huddled together.

"What the fuck is that?" one of the men barked.

Gawa pushed herself away from the trio, but the other man grabbed the tarp and yanked it from her.

"It's a fucking monster!" he shouted.

"Get the fuck away from us!" screamed the woman.

"*You get the fuck away from me!*" Gawa screamed back.

"Oh, no you don't!" snapped the first man, and he reached for her wrist. "We're gonna get rich off this Shift's mantis gland!"

Gawa delved deep into her powers, and the lavender lightning that obeyed her commands lashed out as the man's fingertips came into contact with her marble-rippled skin. Gawa's electricity exploded from her, and the man's body was scorched to a cinder before his companion's eyes.

The woman reached out for him, and the other man yelled, "No!" He grasped her wrist to pull her away, but Gawa's powers chained into the woman's touch and leapt from the first man, pouring into the other two.

The three were dead in an instant.

Gawa ran, leaving the scorched bodies in the street. After only a moment, she arrived at a dead-end with a high wall, the wall that bordered Gate Town. She turned back and followed another street, trying to make her way with the wall in view. Gawa did not encounter any other people in the darkness, and a moment later, she slipped into Gate Town. Several streets farther, she ducked into Red Raven's and took a seat at a lonely corner table to wait for the others; there was more work to be done.

Gawa was dazed, and she sat trying to catch her breath.

Then an old barmaid stepped up and asked her, "What'll it be, dear?"

Back outside, on the southern edge of the peninsula, S'Kay crept along the waterline below the natural topographical rise of the land. During the day, many folks fished from the area, but it was quiet now save for the sounds of the sea.

Through a momentary break in the clouds, the moon's light shined down upon S'Kay, and she noticed that her feather-like protrusions appeared slightly off-color. She shook herself, ruffling them, and a fine cloud of dust lifted from her limbs and torso.

We made quite a mess, she thought to herself.

She continued along the waterfront and soon came to the wall that bordered Gate Town. Instead of following it, she passed beyond the wall and made her way along the edge of the Grey Shallows under the old Oselian gates. The rise of the land where the immovable gate stood cast a dark shadow over S'Kay's path.

After a short while, her trail connected with a level region at the farthest eastern edge of the city's outskirts. S'Kay turned north, entered Gate Town from the outside, and headed toward Red Raven's.

At the eastern tip of the peninsula, Eroli used the same tactic as S'Kay, walking along the water below street level. It took him a while, but eventually and without incident, he reached the airstrip. He made his way toward their underground hideout, but he passed it and climbed up the wall that bordered Gate Town. A few minutes later, he pulled open the door to the tavern.

Lahari ran north from the Tower and ended up near to the old runway, but she suddenly found herself surrounded. In her panic at trying to escape the falling building, she inadvertently ended up in a little open square, and people were approaching her from all directions.

"Well, well, well," one of them sneered, "what have we here?"

"That's a Bio-Shift, mark my words," another added.

"You don't belong here," said a third, and he pulled a knife from his belt.

A few of the folks feared whatever powers Lahari might possess, and they fled from her unique form in terror. The rest drew closer.

Someone said behind her, "It's so ugly."

"But its mantis gland will fetch a pretty bit of coin," added another.

"Kill it," one of the men said. "It's not even human."

It, Lahari thought with a cynical snicker.

Deep in the core of her being, she activated her cosmic energies. They were as easy for Lahari to access as taking a breath. The passive powers of her black hole-like ability were protective, but she now used them to strike out at those who would do her harm.

She stood still at the center of the square.

The gathered rabble charged at her with weapons drawn and murder in their souls, but Lahari's vacuum of energy was like an invisible fog. As the attackers got too close, their life forces were sucked dry before even reaching her. In an instant, a ring of skeletal bodies lay sprawled in the street around Lahari. Those who were behind and watched their companions fall stopped their attack, and they stepped back from her.

Lahari reached even deeper into her powers, and she screamed, as a wave of life-sucking energy radiated out from her. The onslaught vaporized the already wizened bodies at her feet, and as the force of Lahari's void-wave expanded farther, it hit the rest of the villains, who a moment ago thought to cut her down. They fell to the street like living corpses.

She ran, racing down a dark alley toward the entrance of Gate Town. Lahari was alone, but she was alive★

Chapter 30 – Auntie Peg & Ninyani, Part Two

"Hurry up," Auntie Peg urged. Her voice sounded stressed.

Ninyani's hand was in hers as they rushed along.

She made a frustrated noise and asked rhetorically, "Why didn't Ilya fly back with you?"

"Because both of you were upset," Ninyani replied.

Auntie Peg gave his fingers a squeeze. "You're not wrong about that," she said. She then asked him, "You understand what we're requesting of you, right? I can only begin to comprehend how much it means to you, but I agree with Ilya that it's probably the only way, and thank you for your willingness to offer freely."

Auntie Peg continued. "In most people's eyes, anyone who does this is a villain," she stated plainly. "I don't know what people will think afterward."

Ninyani interjected. "I would give anything of mine to help someone else. All of you have helped me so much."

Suddenly Auntie Peg slammed to a halt and extended her arm out to the side in front of Ninyani.

Ahead of them was a thick dust cloud that filled the street.

"I don't like the look of that," she said, and she led him away from it to the southern edge of the Spritehood.

There was a slight drizzle, but the sun was coming up, and the two hustled along above the water. They took a path to the border of the industrial district, and they turned north and followed a street up to Gate Town.

No more violence raged, but buildings were burning, and ahead of them, Auntie Peg saw bodies in the streets. The muffled cries of the dying could be heard in the distance.

"This way!" she said in a singsong voice that sounded nervous. She led Ninyani through the neighborhood and did her best to keep him away from any of the grisly scenes.

"Two blocks," she declared, and as they rounded the last corner, Auntie Peg and Ninyani found their friends.

"...and you've been like a big sister to Ninyani." Dozi stopped telling the story of Tchama's life with her and Ilya, and she looked up. Tears were streaming from her eyes.

The mystic raced over to Auntie Peg and Ninyani. "Is this gonna work?" he asked in a choked voice. He looked back at Tchama.

Ilya was cradling her on the concrete.

Tchama was conscious and writhing in pain. She was missing an arm✪

Chapter 31 – Vion, Part Five

The churning cloud of dust and debris from the fallen Messiah Tower was ahead of Vion, and he rushed toward it. He pulled his shirt collar up over his nose and mouth, squinted his eyes, and entered the dusty storm. Visibility was no more than a few feet, and Vion made his way the best he could in the direction of the devastation. Broken chunks of masonry filled the streets for several blocks as he approached the crumbled temple's base. He stepped over and around pieces that he recognized as recently having been inside the building.

Many of Vion's fellow Messiahs were still at the battle in Gate Town. He wondered how they would survive, and he wished that more of them had shown up from around the city. Near Vion through the cloud, few other people wandered. They looked confused, and they coughed at the dust in the air. He did not recognize anyone he passed, but then a raspy voice called out through the thick fog.

"*Vion!*"

It was an officer that he knew by sight but not name.

"I've been looking for…" the man said, but a fit of coughing interrupted him.

"Easy," Vion replied, but his voice sounded distraught, even to himself. "What happened to the Tower?"

Instead of answering, the officer said, "The Principal Messiah wants to see you, now."

"Where is she?"

More coughing prevented the officer from answering, but he pointed and waved for Vion to follow him. The two headed away from the base of the Tower, and before long, the dust in the air grew thinner and less abrasive.

The officer cleared his throat and said, "She's at the eastern dorm."

Vion nodded and jogged away from the man. He pulled his shirt off his nose and spat the foul taste of the dusty air out of his mouth.

The Messiah's eastern residence was mere blocks from the edge of the peninsula. On its rooftop, the view that looked out over the ocean was spectacular.

Vion saw several of his fellow Messiahs on the top of the building as he approached. When he reached the front, the guards stepped aside and allowed him to enter.

One of them said, "They're on the roof."

Vion nodded and ascended the three stories. He stepped through the door and out into the open air, but the Principal Messiah was not there. The gathered group was *not* looking out over the sprawling sea, instead they were staring at the massive gray cloud where their temple used to stand.

The sun was starting to rise and a chilly rain began to pelt down on them.

"Where is the Principal Messiah?" Vion asked.

"She said to tell you to clean up and meet her at the prime house."

Without a word, Vion descended into the communal residence. He set out a fresh pair of clothes and entered the showers.

Someone else was already in one of the stalls, and Vion cranked on the faucet of another. He stripped off his dusty clothes and stepped under the water.

After a moment, the other shower stopped and a voice said, "That's you, Vion, right?"

"Yes, what do you want?" he asked while scrubbing his hair.

"The question is," the other person replied, "what does *she* want?"

Vion did not understand. "What does who want?"

"Our leader," the voice oozed, "what do you suppose the Principal Messiah wants?"

"I couldn't pretend to imagine," Vion responded in a dismissive tone. He was nearly finished washing and wanted to be left alone. The communal housing tended to make people feel overly comfortable, and Vion was not in the mood for a discussion about whatever his fellow Messiah was insinuating, especially not while they were both naked.

"There's a lotta dead Messiahs," the other person commented.

Vion bristled. "We are at war," he replied in a stony tone.

The voice was not finished. "A lot die in war."

"Yes," Vion agreed. He was clean and ready to get out of the shower. "Is there some point to this discussion?" he asked, but he received no reply.

Vion pulled back the curtain. No one else was in the showers with him. The floor was wet from someone's feet, and another shower curtain was now pulled back, but he was alone.

Within the hour, Vion was below the executive residence of the Principal Messiah. The prime house was in an old Oselian watchtower room that was built into the side of a massive piece of concrete wall. A major portion of it had collapsed at some point in the past, and the only access up to the prime house was via an external elevator. It descended when Vion came into view, as if the Principal Messiah was waiting for him. He opened the lift's door, stepped inside, and shut it again. It began to rise.

Vion gazed out over the city, shocked at the way it now looked without its prominent feature thrusting toward the sky. The gray cloud of dust looked like an unnatural shadow of the clouds above.

The elevator reached the top, and the door opened.

Vion stepped out of it and into the luxurious apartment of the Messiah leader. She had been in the position for barely a year, and there was no way of knowing how many of Vion's fellow Messiahs were now dead in the streets or murdered by Shifts. He gritted his teeth and set his jaw, ready for whatever reprimand the Principal Messiah held in store for him.

To his surprise and confusion, she was dressed in lacy lingerie and was sprawled out on her bed with a come-hither expression in her eyes.

"You kept me waiting," she teased in a husky voice.

Vion did not understand.

The woman got onto her hands and knees and crept towards the edge of the bed with her mouth open and lips pouty. "Well, don't just stand there," she whispered, and the Principal Messiah reached out to Vion from across the room.

"Milady?" he gasped.

Then the floor between them exploded with purple electricity★

Chapter 32 – Sacrifice

The Messiah who had been chasing Tchama was now dead in the street. An eldritch bolt of orange energy came out of nowhere from an unseen Shift. It collided with the woman and killed her instantly. Her two short swords were on the pavement beside her corpse. The radiant blast was powerful enough to destroy the Messiah, but it also grazed Tchama and left her utterly ruined.

Ilya held her writhing body. One of the young woman's arms was entirely gone and all that remained was the scorched and gory stump of her shoulder. The burn stretched up the side of her neck and down onto her ribs where a huge chunk of flesh from her side was missing; the bones beneath were exposed.

Dozi was beside them, holding Tchama's remaining hand. She looked up at Auntie Peg with tears streaming from her eyes.

Tchama was gritting her teeth and groaning.

Ninyani touched Dozi's shoulder and knelt beside her. He took Tchama's hand from hers and looked into the injured woman's eyes.

She stared at him.

"They say if you eat this," Ninyani told her in a quiet voice, as he reached into his pocket, "you'll get better. I don't want you to die." He pulled out his little coin purse, opened it, and withdrew the photonova gland that was hidden inside. Tears began to stream from his eyes, and he repeated himself. "I don't want you to die, Tchama."

Auntie Peg and the mystic were the only two who had ever seen a photonova gland in person, and for a moment, the others did not know what Ninyani was holding.

"Open your mouth," Auntie Peg commanded Tchama, as Theolan extended her a thermos of water. "Swallow this, now."

Tchama could barely respond but managed to obey. She gulped the tiny gem down her throat and drank as Auntie Peg poured a little water into her mouth.

Nothing happened.

Tchama continued to grind her teeth and squirm in her suffering.

The others looked at Auntie Peg in dismay.

"Maybe it was too old," she whispered.

Then Tchama sucked in air through her teeth, and she let out a horrible scream that made everyone jump. She gasped and clenched into a ball with her knees close to her chest. For a moment, she twisted in Ilya's embrace. Then all at once she stopped and her eyes flashed open.

To everyone's amazement, the gruesome wound that stretched from her neck down to her side healed before their eyes and became unblemished skin again. Tchama's arm, however, did not grow back. A fresh layer of epidermis grew, but the bones and muscles and the entire limb remained gone.

Tchama took a breath, pushed herself up to a seated position, and she blinked a few times at them. She looked down at the place where her arm used to be, before turning her gaze to Ninyani.

"Tha... thank you," she stammered, and her eyes filled with tears. Tchama brought her remaining hand to her face, dropped her head, and sobbed.

The others soothed her, and she accepted their comfort. It took time, but when the shock of it all subsided, she looked up and wrapped her single arm around Ninyani. She kissed his forehead and he hugged her tight.

"I'm glad you're okay," he said to her. He pulled back, looked at her armless shoulder, and asked in a quiet voice, "Does it hurt?"

"No," Tchama replied, "it almost feels like it's still there, but there's no pain." She touched it.

"You're a Messiah now," Dozi whispered.

"Don't call me that!" Tchama snapped. "I'm not one of those monsters! I would never have done this, and now that I'm *not* on the verge of dying," she wailed, as she looked around at them, "I feel so guilty! I should have just died! What kind of life is this? Now I'm one of *them!*" Tears spilled from her eyes again.

"I am, too," Auntie Peg replied with a kind smile, "and I became one by choice. You have nothing to feel guilty about. Do you hear me, Tchama? You are not guilty of anything except living."

Tchama broke down in sobs, and several of the others cried along with her. They eventually helped her to her feet, and they all entered the mystic's home.

When the group was settled, Dozi stated, "We need an alternate term."

"I agree," added Auntie Peg. "I'm an ex-Messiah, but Tchama, you've never been one. We'll have to come up with something different. What did you all call Agrell?" She looked around at the group. "I know she was raised like me, to eventually be a Messiah, but she didn't live for a single day as one."

"I don't know," Dozi replied. "We didn't call her anything."

"Except for *Messiah* a few times," Ilya admitted with an apologetic grin.

"We'll come up with something for you, Tchama," Dozi declared, "a term that fits."

Tchama looked at Ninyani and again she pulled him close and hugged the boy with her one arm. She repeated herself, "Thank you. You really are part of our family."

Ninyani's expression indicated that he suddenly remembered something, and he looked around the room with a furrowed brow.

"Where's Lahari?" he asked✪

Chapter 33 – The Beginning

Lahari launched herself up through the hole in the ceiling that Gawa blasted with her purple lightning, and she landed between Vion and the scantily-clad Principal Messiah. They were already stunned from the explosion, but the two of them were even more shocked by Lahari's physical appearance. Her unique blue scaly skin and black quills made her look armored, and her appearance seemed monstrous to the two Messiahs.

"*What the fuck are you?!*" the woman shrieked from her bed.

S'Kay and Gawa leapt up through the hole in the floor. The bird-woman landed to one side of Lahari, and the Biological Shift who looked like living stone landed to her other.

Eroli climbed up after them and growled. He shook his fur and extended his claws to their full length.

"Kill those fucking freaks!" the Principal Messiah screamed at Vion, as S'Kay leapt at the bed.

The Principal Messiah tried to back away, but she became tangled in the sheets, and S'Kay wrapped her arms around the woman. Many of her feathers caused tiny wounds all over the Principal Messiah's body, and she let out a single scream, as the energies within S'Kay began to liquefy her flesh from her bones. Her body shook violently, but that only made her melting meat dissolve faster. Green bones protruded from her destroyed corpse.

"You're the scum I've been looking for!" Vion bellowed, but instead of attacking them, he took a fearful step back.

S'Kay climbed off the slimy green skeleton of the Principal Messiah, and the four Biological Shifts stared at Vion.

"Keep away from me, you murderers! Stay back!"

Eroli dove for him and the two collided. Vion gasped and Eroli let out a wheeze.

Gawa froze. "*No!*" she wailed.

Both Vion and Eroli struck killing blows.

Eroli's chest was caved in, buckled like dented metal. His eyes were wide in wild horror. He struggled to take shallow and ragged breaths.

Vion, however, was motionless. The color was no longer in his eyes. Then the hue began to disappear from his skin, as well. The

High Truth Seeker of the Messiahs became little more than a crystalline shell of his former self.

Eroli's claws slid from Vion's chest, as the two men fell to the ground.

Vion's body shattered.

Gawa rushed to her fellow Biological Shift and fell to her knees. "Eroli," she whispered, as he released his final gasping breath. Gawa let out a pitiful sob and began to cry.

S'Kay knelt beside Gawa and sorrowfully sighed, as tears streamed down her feathered cheeks.

The old Oselian viewing platform looked over Teshon Harbor, and Lahari stepped up to gaze out at the panoramic view. Then she turned back to Gawa and S'Kay, and Lahari said, "This is just the beginning."★

Book Three is now available!
"THE MANTIS CORRUPTION"

"The Mantis Corruption is actual nightmare
fuel not for anyone with a weak stomach."
- Claire Rosalind

Adam Andrews Johnson